ROSA'S VERY OWN PERSONAL REVOLUTION

Eric Dupont

ROSA'S VERY OWN PERSONAL REVOLUTION

Translated from the French by
Peter McCambridge

QC FICTION

Revision: Katherine Hastings
Proofreading: Elizabeth West, Arielle Aaronson
Book design: Folio infographie
Cover & logo: Maison 1608 by Solisco
Cover art: Kai McCall
Fiction editor: Peter McCambridge

Copyright © 2013 Marchand de feuilles
Originally published under the title *La Logeuse*
by Marchand de feuilles, 2013 (first edition 2006) (Montréal, Québec)
Translation copyright © Peter McCambridge

ISBN 978-1-77186-288-2 pbk; 978-1-77186-289-9 epub; 978-1-77186-290-5 pdf

Legal Deposit, 3rd quarter 2022
Bibliothèque et Archives nationales du Québec
Library and Archives Canada

Published by QC Fiction, an imprint of Baraka Books
Printed and bound in Québec

TRADE DISTRIBUTION & RETURNS
Canada - UTP Distribution: UTPdistribution.com
United States & World - Independent Publishers Group: IPGbook.com

We acknowledge the financial support for translation and promotion of the Société de développement des entreprises culturelles (SODEC), the Government of Québec tax credit for book publishing administered by SODEC, the Government of Canada, and the Canada Council for the Arts.

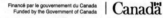

CHAPTER 1

Flotsam

A MOTHER AND DAUGHTER walk along the deserted shore, among the shrieking gulls and the limp seaweed. Standing in her rubber boots, the little girl leans into the west wind, stretching out her arms and letting herself be buffeted by the gusts. Set against the blue of the raging sea, rocking back on her heels, Rosa Ost, still blissfully unaware that she's about to learn the past tense, looks on as the two red bows securing her ginger braids dance in the squall, and she thinks to herself that the wind will keep her balanced like this until her dying day. On the Gaspé Peninsula, the wind can be a crutch to lean on.

"Rosa, you're gonna fall in," her mother warns her. "One day the wind's gonna die down and you'll end up

9

flat on your bagg in the freezing water. Do you really want to ggatch your death on the beach? You'll be the end of me! It's bad enough your father ended up in a watery grave!"

Terese Ost, armed with a bucket and spade, is teaching her eight-year-old daughter to fish for sea urchins. On this Sunday afternoon, they've left behind the peninsula of Notre-Dame-du-Cachalot to venture out onto the sandy point. The point has the best views of this hamlet at the end of the world, a tiny village forgotten by God and all of humankind. It's clear from the primitive, rickety architecture of the wood and shingle homes that the occupants didn't intend to linger here long either. And yet they've called it home since 1840. An image of this seaswept scene will fill Rosa's eyes on the evening they close for the very last time.

But what she doesn't know is that she still has a long life ahead of her, a very long life indeed.

And so it was here in the village that had sprung up on the far side of a sand dune that, on May 20, 1980, Rosa Ost, the only daughter of Terese Ost, fair-to-middling trade unionist and first-rate Scrabble player, was born. It is the tragic fate of this child that will be of interest to us throughout this tale of long journeys and longer lives, of impossible deaths, unwavering prophecies, and unsettling dreams. As was the case with many of the children in Notre-Dame-du-Cachalot, the little girl was fortunate enough not to have known her father. It was in fact a custom in the village to limit contact between children and their fathers as much as possible. The decision had been made shortly before Rosa was born, following a series of unfortunate events that had weighed heavily on the mental health of all too many infants or, indeed, cost them their lives. The villagers had eventually realized that children were dying from malnutrition, abuse, or simply being left outside in conditions better suited to penguins, while in the care of their absent-minded fathers. Which is not to say that the fathers in the village were any less attentive or attached to their offspring than elsewhere; they were just distracted, that's all. Rosa had managed to outlive her father because fate had had the decency to lose him at sea while he was out herring fishing one misty day in May 1980, when the lighthouse at Cape Cachalot had inexplicably gone out, never to come on again. The day after the wreck, debris from the boat belonging to Rosa's father washed up on the shingle beaches of Notre-Dame-du-Cachalot, at the foot of the conked-out lighthouse, at the end of the peninsula where the little girl would go for Saturday afternoon strolls, still looking, years after the disaster, for flotsam that would have served as a relic of the father she had not known and that her mother refused to discuss. All she had of him now were half his genes and the pang of regret she felt at not having known him. Terese had destroyed every last photo that might have helped Rosa explore her past. Only by observing her mother's features did Rosa manage to piece together a mental image of her late father. Her red hair, blue eyes, and easy gait must have come from him. As for the rest, try as it might, her imagination was none the wiser.

On that Saturday afternoon spent fishing for sea urchins, Terese and her sole contribution to future generations made a peculiar discovery. A huge block of ice had drifted in on the tide during the night, slathered in seaweed. They could make out a purple spot at the centre of the translucent iceberg and resolved to get to the bottom of it. By hook and by crook, they managed to drag the frozen monolith back home, where they waited for the heat to do its work. After hours spent dabbing at puddles with bath towels then wringing them out over the kitchen sink, they had the surprise of their lives when they discovered, clinging to a lifebuoy from the *Empress of Ireland*—the luxury liner that foundered off Rimouski in the spring of 1914—a shrivelled little old lady, clad in purple velvet.

Was she a victim of the shipwreck, or just some woman who had drowned near Quebec City only for her body to get caught up in a lifebuoy drifting off the coast of Rimouski? No one would ever know. The freezing waters of the Gulf of St. Lawrence had prevented the body from putrefying, and it wasn't until Terese had set her down in front of the oil furnace for eight days straight that the woman's expression began to soften. It was another couple of weeks before she could pick herself up, and longer still before she could speak again. When at last her jaw allowed her to emerge from more than seventy years of silence, she exclaimed in a voice that seemed to come from beyond the grave: "In like a lion, out like a lamb." Little Rosa, at barely eight years old, had just learned her first proverb. "And to thingg I was loogging for sea urchins!" Terese exclaimed.

The sea had claimed a father from Rosa and given her a grandmother. The little girl, as anyone would agree, had come out on top.

Distinctly unimpressed by the old lady's strange ways, Terese named her Zenaida, took her under her wing (since she was entirely without friends or family), and declared her honorary grandmother to her daughter, a task that Zenaida went about with every ounce of grace and valour that she could muster. Zenaida was afflicted with a rare form of colour blindness that allowed her to see only certain shades of violet and mauve. The old woman, anxious to avoid appearing in public wearing ill-matched or garish clothes, made a point of only wearing colours that recalled a blossoming lilac, which happened to be the village's floral emblem. And since she was a talented seamstress, she began to dress Terese and Rosa in what had been the height of fashion at the turn of the twentieth century. Before Zenaida came into her life, Terese had found only one valid reason to get dressed in the morning: because otherwise she would be naked. Zenaida brought the elegance of bygone days to their home, along with the wisdom of her proverbs. Nothing was ever known of her true identity. Terese had named her Zenaida after a late aunt. As the old dear put it so eloquently herself: "Long ways, long lies."

Notre-Dame-du-Cachalot, despite all you may have heard to the contrary, embodies the least-known culmination of the Marxist-inspired socialist political ideal. The phenomenon may be unknown to us, but that's not to say it doesn't exist. The men and women behind this experiment in political economy wouldn't have had it any other way. In the 1970s, when the bankruptcies of the planned economies of Eastern Europe were being written in the stars in blazing letters, a handful of goateed men from the Ministry of GLUM (Grey, Lifeless, and Unloved Municipalities) sat down and came up with a plan to save Marxist ideology. It involved creating irrefutable proof, in the form of a village, that a socialist paradise was within reach, and could be achieved without subjecting its residents to regrettable Stalinist-style persecution. The day when all believed communism to be dead and buried, the day when the Golden Arches cast their glow over even Havana and Pyongyang, the day when the last party cell disappeared for lack of members, that day the truth would be revealed about Notre-Dame-du-Cachalot, and the whole world, chastened by the error of its ways, would turn the tide of history and reproduce, on every continent, the success of that little village on the Gaspé Peninsula.

It was easy for GLUM to create the conditions required for an experiment that would one day save Marxism from the wringer of imperialism. First of all, the wise men agreed that the people who lived in the village must never know that they were part of an experiment. In their opinion, the October Revolution and other proletarian movements owed their failure largely to the fact that revolutionaries had shouted their intentions from the rooftops. The people, for whom the promised fruits of revolt were a long time coming, went on to swell the ranks of the counter-revolution. It seemed more sensible to introduce the project on the quiet, like a parent fibbing to a child who won't stop asking, "Are we there yet?"

Tourist brochures the world over couldn't have been clearer: Notre-Dame-du-Cachalot wasn't worth visiting. Its sole attraction stood just outside the village: three enormous piles of stone and shingle towering at least thirty metres in height. From a distance, they looked like three pyramids. Dubbed "The Three Sisters" by the villagers, the mounds were explained on a woodworm-riddled panel by the side of the road.

"Discovered by the first eighteenth-century settlers, these piles of stone are all that remains of a structure erected to a deity by the Mi'kmaq. Legend has it, the Mi'kmaq built these three stone pyramids following a promise made by Glooskap—the supreme being who gives meaning to all—that, upon catching sight of them, the white man who arrived from the Atlantic would realize that the land was already occupied and keep his distance."

The truth was much more grisly. Each of the "sisters" in fact hid the bones of an unfortunate individual from the village that an angry mob had slain in an outpouring of rage. And so it was that three ghosts haunted Notre-Dame-du-Cachalot.

April 27, 1942: Comrade Baptiste Deloursin, 35 years old, Scorpio, whose early-blooming lilac had infuriated the rest of the village, was stoned to death while crying "No! No! No!" on the very spot where the first sister stands today. His efforts to flee to the covered bridge that links the peninsula to the rest of the continent were in vain.

November 1, 1987: Comrade Madeleine Barachois, 55 years old, Libra, was in turn hunted down and butchered while crying "No! No! No!" The proud owner of a Christmas cactus that, as if by magic, never failed to bloom the day before each and every December blizzard, she had taken to forecasting the worst of the snowstorms. On that fateful morning, Madeleine had boasted that her cactus would be blooming early that year. The villagers, incensed at the thought of an early blizzard, concluded that the poor woman not only looked forward to but was in fact responsible for the storms and, confusing causation with correlation, they gave birth to the second sister under a hail of stones. Madeleine Barachois perished as she tried to flee with her beloved cactus. Despite the disappearance of the ill-fated succulent, the first snowstorm of winter 1987 arrived as per usual, on December 8, the Feast of the Immaculate Conception.

October 30, 1995: Comrade Kevin Crachin, 8 years old, Aries, awoke from a nightmare calling out, "Peter Piper picked a peck of pickled pepper," all trace of the locals' traditionally swallowed consonants gone. The villagers were fit to be tied as they awoke to the sound of the clear and precise plosives. The first stones shattered the ground-floor window of the Crachin home and, despite the stream of invective let loose by the mother, who stumbled from one villager to the next, clad only in a simple floral nightgown, imploring them to stop the unwarranted punishment while the little boy escaped with his teddy bear and made for the covered bridge, there, lurking in the shadows, a few of the villagers lay in wait for him. He was struck on the forehead just as he figured his nighttime run had brought him salvation. Aristide Nordet, the baker, finished off the last in the Crachin line by casting a stone that hit the back of the boy's perspiring head with a thud. Kevin perished in turn for his inexcusable act of phonetic treason. As with the others, his final cries were lost to the eastern sky: "No! No! No!"

Two morals can be drawn from these three stories: One, all kinds of things get pinned on the First Nations. And, two, gardening and a fondness for language can both prove fatal, if you're not careful.

In this godforsaken backwater, where the frozen expanses of the Gulf of St. Lawrence served as the sole horizon, two industries reigned supreme: paper and Boredom. West of the village stood the Petticoat Paper Mill. Closed since 1980 following the collapse of the world paper market, the mill now stood empty; the eight hundred workers it had employed at the height of production had been relieved of their duties, still waiting twenty years later for the company to start up again. Bailouts were promised election after election, but never materialized. At first, the people of Notre-Dame-du-Cachalot were indignant and demanded to be put to work at once. They voiced their discontent to management, who fobbed them off with the usual:

"The Atlanta Petticoat Paper Company understands the frustrations of the people of Our Lady of the Cachalot and stresses that its primary objective is to see production levels in its Canadian facilities return to the levels of

1976. However, it must be understood that high salaries are detrimental to productivity at our Canadian mills and the Company is on occasion obliged to focus production on mills located in countries where obstacles to trade are less substantial. Our Board of Directors has made it a priority to reopen the Petticoat Eastern Canada division as soon as the world paper market permits."

At Atlanta Petticoat Paper headquarters, they'd been photocopying the same press release for each of their Canadian mills for the past twenty years. Apart from the name of the town, each time not so much as a comma had changed. Only the means of delivery was different. Up until 1984, someone would be sent up from the Montreal office to read the edict aloud. The same company rep, who had learned his trade at the finest business schools, travelled the length and breadth of Eastern Canada, from village to village, from haystack to haystack, to make the announcement. For his troubles, he got a navy blue suit, a salary commensurate with his functions, and travel expenses. After 1984, Petticoat Eastern Canada moved its Montreal office to Seattle, where it became Petticoat Western, much to the delight of its lumbago-suffering employees, who had spent half the year shovelling snow from the paved driveways of their tiny Montreal homes. The company rep followed the rest of the team, finding new work announcing clear-cuts in the forests of the Rocky Mountains.

After that, it had befallen the Quebec government to give the people of Notre-Dame-du-Cachalot the bad news. This suited the pen-pushers at the Ministry of

GLUM perfectly. Now they could exercise greater control over the village without the risk of the Petticoat Paper Company turning up at any moment to announce the reopening of the Notre-Dame-du-Cachalot mill.

The village's favourite sport was Scrabble. On that August evening in the year 2000, Terese Ost, retired trade unionist, had just scored ten points, plus fifty bonus points, for using up all seven of the tiles that had been taunting her from their little wooden rack. Aunt Zenaida wrote down sixty points for her host.

Rosa, now twenty years old, scooped four letters out of the little pink velvet bag that Aunt Zenaida had sewn for their long Scrabble games. Terese, lost to gloomy reminiscences, stared out the window that the wind was threatening to rip clear of its frame and, as though possessed by an evil spirit, exclaimed: "Who on earth is going to ggome get us out of this unsavoury mess?" At the very moment Rosa looked down at the four little tiles nestling in the still-chubby palm of her hand, a flash of lightning lit up the letters R-O-S-E in a fleeting, uncompromising glare. Since Rosa used the first E of ENDURED, her stroke of inspiration was rewarded with only four points. Had she used the final E, a double letter score would have left her with five. But Rosa doesn't count. She's not the calculating type. She's just happy to find somewhere for her little wooden tiles.

ROS ENDURED

But let us leave the three women to their fun and rummage around a little more in their pasts. Terese had made something of a project of her daughter's education. She was one of those people who is utterly convinced that, when all is said and done, very little of what we do in life is for ourselves, and the most precious distillate of our experience should be shared with as many people as humanly possible. All too often, she had been advised to think of herself, to experience the world rather than try to change it. "Charity begins at home," the old woman would tell her. "And dignity? Where does dignity begin?" she would reply with a smile, whenever she bothered to reply. Revolutionaries, priests, grey nuns, altruists of all sorts, Christ himself, and more than a few members of Greenpeace adhere to this same school of thought. And their children are no exception.

The predisposition is genetic.

Little Rosa's education had started the day her birth certificate was filed with the government. It was to Rosa Luxemburg that the child owed her dated, unfashionable name, Terese seeking to find a new body for the murdered revolutionary. Like any self-respecting daughter of the head of the Paper Workers' Union, the little girl got wind of age-old grudges in the village with every passing day. As it happened, the villagers blamed Terese for the paper mill closing. She had, the older workers maintained, overplayed their hand. Petticoat's actions looked to that particular lumpenproletariat more like divine retribution than a profit-oriented business strategy. Resentment was served up morning, noon, and night, especially in the winter. Rosa quickly grew accustomed to it, which was just as well, since she was destined to live with those people. Little Rosa Ost's earliest reading materials had included Marx's *Capital* and *Political Writings*, which didn't prevent her, just like any other child, from taking refuge in a future that beckoned with a smile. One thing that associates all red writing with a propensity to gather dust is that reading it makes people believe in the future. You can't be a communist and a pessimist, too. How cute she looked, sitting at the table in the huge Gaspé kitchen as her mother finished deboning a chicken and Aunt Zenaida knitted her mauve woollen socks, reading out loud, stumbling over the words, in that wonderful local accent of hers that was entirely oblivious to the K sound, passages that she didn't understand a single word of: "The masses were up to the challenge, and out of this 'defeat' they have forged a lingg in the chain of historigg defeats, which is the pride and strength of international socialism. That is why future viggtories will spring from this 'defeat.'"

"Well put. Isn't that right, Rosa?"

"Yes, Mother."

"A bird in the hand is worth two in the bush!" bleated the grandmother.

The old woman was inclined to greet any passage from Marx, Lenin, Luxemburg, or the others with that old proverb or, on holy days, with "If youth but knew, if old age but could," without so much as glancing up from her knitting. While Terese derived some solace from that passage plucked from the writings of Luxemburg, the comfort it brought to Rosa came purely from the musicality of its language. And so it was that mother and daughter both considered the text to be a keystone of their relationship. Each night after supper, two hours were valiantly given over to revolutionary texts. As the seasons passed, Marx gave way to Trotsky, then Trotsky to Lenin, to whom the long winter months were devoted to preserve the text's Soviet feel.

And, of course, there was Scrabble. Hunched over in silent contemplation of the seven varnished wood letters, they expressed themselves solely through the words they chanced upon. We find them once again on that August evening in 2000. Aunt Zenaida had put down the five-letter word I-D-I-O-T, taking care to lay her tiles atop the dark blue Triple Letter Score square for eight points.

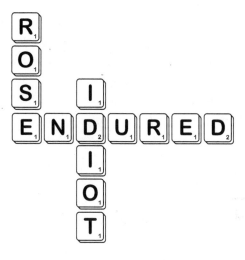

"Reminds me of the time that Danish man ggame by," Terese said.

"You'd need an S at the end for that," her daughter chipped in.

The three generations burst out laughing.

Who could forget the time that Danish man paid them a visit? Once again, we must look up from the scene and return to the source of the laughter. Madeleine Saint-Trombone, a devoted civil servant from the Ministry of GLUM, had followed in the footsteps of the calamitous Petticoat messenger. She had been slightly underpaid and slightly underdressed compared to her predecessor, but her lack of sophistication only made her more relatable to the villagers who had been forced out of commission. For the first few years, she had made the schlep to Notre-Dame-du-Cachalot once a year to reassure the villagers of the government's plans for regional development.

Her message remained more or less unchanged. The government was actively seeking fresh investment to get the paper mill up and running again. Occasionally she would stall for time, announcing that a Franco-Italian consortium had expressed a vague interest or that a Sino-Japanese industrial conglomerate had been making woolly promises, all of which she naturally made up from start to finish in order to pacify the unemployed proletariat. Her task had become easier with time, since those clamouring the loudest to be chained to a production line gradually left the region to find work for their idle hands. The people who stayed behind continued to protest, but their hearts were no longer in it.

One day, however, the good woman from GLUM turned up unannounced with a Germano-Danish delegation tasked with studying the area's wind power potential. Eating nothing but fried herring, for two months the three delegates with long, fair hair measured air streams by the gulf using strange and very expensive equipment. Then they shut themselves away for two weeks in an abandoned shingled home that had been put at their disposal. No one ever saw the scientists go in or out of their makeshift research centre. They were too busy drawing plans, making calculations, extrapolating tangents, and predicting air movements as they had already done in their home countries, dotting the North Sea with wind farms that were the envy of the entire world. The Quebec government, too, began to dream of tending to its own crop of giant white daisies spread across the Gulf of St. Lawrence. After two weeks of hard work, the three tall and rather lanky individuals emerged from their self-imposed lockdown to announce that the villagers would be the first to know the results of their research. The people of Notre-Dame-du-Cachalot were expected at the parish hall that same evening. The news spread quickly, and the windswept villagers soon found themselves jostling for one of the orange plastic chairs. Outside, a gale blew an octave or two higher than the drone of the impatient crowd that filled the huge room amid decorative pink trellises and paintings of hulking ships, fishing scenes, and bird colonies.

On the stage, five microphones had been set up around a table at which, from left to right, sat Dr. Peder Pedersen, co-director of the Royal Institute for Wind Energy Research in Copenhagen; Professor Ingeborg Borgman, his German counterpart from Stralsund University; their cook and personal interpreter who followed them everywhere and insisted on travelling under the cover of anonymity; then finally the local mayor (elected for life) and president of the Notre-Dame-du-Cachalot Chamber of Commerce, Nicéphore Duressac; and GLUM civil servant Madeleine Saint-Trombone. The mayor spoke first:

"My fellow citizens, it is with great pleasure that we find ourselves here this evening, awaiting the results of the study into our charming village's suitability as a wind farm site. The projeggt we have been waiting on for years has at last reached its end, and our esteemed guests from Europe are ggeen to present their ggonggglusions to us all. First of all, I would ligge to thanggg you on their behalf for the ggordial welggome you eggstended to them over the past number of weeggs as they agreed, in return for the modest sum of three million dollars, to study our air streams with a view to proposing a wind farm projeggt to the government that would ggreate more than ten permanent jobs in our region, where they are sorely needed. I will now pass the migge to Doggtor Peder Pedersen, ggo-direggtor of the Royal Institute for Wind Energy Research in Ggopenhagen."

Madeleine Saint-Trombone pinched her thigh hard to stifle a giggle. The honourable mayor had, as everyone could hear, a strong local accent, which was only natural since he'd never once ventured beyond his mist-covered dune. As mentioned earlier, the people of Notre-Dame-du-Cachalot were known throughout the province for their inability to pronounce the K sound, almost invariably replacing it with a G sound that was easier on the palate. In the village, pronouncing one's Ks was associated with Montreal, and therefore with treachery and perdition. Though the odd little habit gave the villagers a sense of belonging to the bleak and hostile Gaspé Peninsula, more than anything it left others wondering why they seemed to have a permanent cold. In France, rumour held this to be true, due to the hostile climate that prevailed there nine months of the year, hence the popular belief that Gaspé was in fact pronounced Kaspé, a conviction that became so entrenched that soon there was no point in trying to set the record straight.

Dr. Pedersen, who had been dozing off at the far end of the table, gave a start upon hearing his name and began to rummage through a pile of papers stained with tartar sauce and cooking oil. He began to deliver the fruits of his research in his native tongue. Dr. Pedersen knew only one word in his hosts' language—"*malheureusement*"—a term that already covered much of what he had to say about the region. Those in attendance had to listen carefully, since the simultaneous translation was a two-part process. First came the scientist's voice, low and soft-spoken, full of ø and K sounds, emanating from behind his ill-trimmed beard. Then the translator-cum-cook simultaneously translated Pedersen's words into English, which Madeleine Saint-Trombone—who had emerged fluent in both English and French from her first marriage to a Vermont beekeeper, before he'd left her for a younger, more honeyed voice—then had to interpret into French for the audience. Fortunately for all concerned, the researcher was disconcertingly concise. At the end of this chain of Babylonian proportions, Madeleine Saint-Trombone exclaimed:

"It's very windy here!"

The silence weighed heavily on the parish hall. Rosa heard her adoptive grandmother muttering in a voice clear enough to be picked up by half the audience:

"In the kingdom of the blind, the one-eyed man is king."

Visibly uncomfortable, Ms. Saint-Trombone began applauding to drown out the silence, which could now be measured by the ton. The rest of the audience followed her lead. Satisfied by the effect their declaration had had, the three Europeans smiled, stood up, waved to the crowd, and left the hall, followed by the civil servant.

They would never set foot in Notre-Dame-du-Cachalot again. They're still travelling to this day, being paid small fortunes to tell the people of Mali that their country is sandy, the people of Siberia that their homeland is a little on the chilly side, and the people of Brazil that their climate might be well suited to growing coffee.

Back in Terese Ost's kitchen, the laughter died down. Terese's letters clattered onto the Scrabble board: C-A-K-E. Fifteen points. Desserts can be so rewarding.

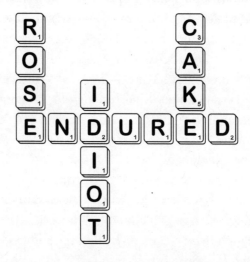

"And I won't be sharing this one!" said Rosa, referring to the embarrassing birthday that still lived long in every villager's memory.

The day her daughter turned nine, Terese had invited all the children in Rosa's class over for a birthday party that had taken her weeks to prepare. The good socialist might have been unemployed, but she was far from idle, having kept herself busy with all kinds of projects since the paper mill had closed. Aside from the household chores, which Zenaida took care of, there was plenty to keep an erstwhile unionist busy in rural Quebec. She worked hard to keep the memory of the union alive and, against all odds, to continue to spread the red ideology with the zeal of a Carmelite nun. For Rosa's birthday, she fetched from the attic the red Paper Workers' Union flags and covered the ceiling of each room with little red stars. "And there's Orion," she said to herself on her way out of the living room. Of the twenty-four young guests who were invited, not one showed up, and the enormous golden-brown cake, shaped like the hammer and sickle, seemed to taunt the three women as they stood around the lavishly decorated table. There was no need for an investigation into the motives of Rosa's classmates. The truth was simple: Of the twenty-four mothers of the children invited, a good half of them still silently cursed Terese Ost and her union, blaming them for the Petticoat Paper Co. mill closing. The others, who remained untainted by festering resentment, had decided to keep their offspring at home so that they would not have to witness the Marxist madness that Terese Ost had descended into ever since her dreams had fallen apart.

The card invited "Rosa's comrades to come celebrate her ninth birthday at 36 Des Crevettiers at noon on May 20." By three o'clock that afternoon, it had become clear that no one would be coming. Needless to say, most little girls that age would have reacted very differently to being so horribly shunned. We know several who would have burst into tears then run off to hide in their rooms for days, spinning into a spiral of depression and rejection that would have inevitably led to illicit drugs or a career as a teacher. We know others who, cut to the quick by such an insult, would have allowed the uncompromising matron within them to grow. And yet the magic of her genes won out, and our little Rosa reacted in keeping with how she'd been brought up. Zenaida tried to defuse the situation as calmly as possible. "Every cloud has a silver lining." To which little Rosa replied, "If the mountain won't come to Muhammad, then Muhammad must go to the mountain."

And so it was. Rosa cut the huge cake into twenty-four perfectly equal slices and set them on little cardboard plates, each with a decorative red star in the middle. She lined the plates up on three serving trays, put on her windbreaker, and went with Zenaida and her mother to hand deliver a share of the cake to the guests. Shamefaced at not even having had the decency to decline the invitation, each child had meekly eaten every last crumb of their share of the socialist dessert, as the three women looked on.

"Thank you, Mrs. Ost."

"Don't mention it, comrade."

From that day forward, a feeling of guilt, tinged with a sugary aftertaste, washed over the parents of Notre-Dame-du-Cachalot every May 20, simply because they hadn't allowed their children the pleasure of attending an innocent birthday party. The sickly sweet and rather lumpy icing was imprinted on the memory of every child, a regret that would never leave them. For the rest of their lives, every time they swallowed a piece of cake, they would have to choke back a sob of shame. The dessert had been Terese's final act of revenge, confirming the rumour that, just like sweets, socialism, too, can sometimes be a little hard to stomach.

After the memorable gathering during which a bearded Dane had revealed to the people of the village that they lived in a rather windy part of the world, Mayor Duressac scrambled for a way to calm the audience. "At least we still have our source of Boredom," he said, trying to sound reassuring. An approving rumble rose up from the mass of villagers as they left the parish hall by the main door, braving an unbelievable west wind as they returned to their homes.

Duressac knew that he could always count on Boredom, the mainstay of the village's economy, to quell the impatience of folks who, like a fading movie star, had seen better days. It must be said that the Boredom sourced from Notre-Dame-du-Cachalot was known the world over as the purest to be found anywhere on earth. In fact, the naturally occurring deposit of Boredom still employed a score of villagers and could pride itself on having never experienced a single dip in production since a villager first stumbled upon the geyser in 1971. The happy discovery had followed the sad loss of Robert Caplan's wife, whom Caplan had insisted on burying in his backyard. It was while digging his wife's grave that he discovered the powerful underground source. Alerted by his shouts, the rest of the village came running to the scene, where they recognized the distinctive odour of Boredom. Since a nor'easter happened to be blowing a gale that day, a Boston billionaire got wind of the discovery and, smelling a profit, bought the entire deposit for next to nothing, exporting Boredom from Notre-Dame-du-Cachalot. Life in the hamlet was never the same again. The village's name was heard all the way around the world, without anyone really being able to say exactly where it was. The Bostonian businessman shipped the precious gas to Central America, where it was distilled into concentrate, poured into elegant spray bottles that had been decorated by well-known artists, and marketed as PUR ENNUI®. Despite the eye-watering prices, buyers around the world snapped up the bottles, each bearing the much sought-after appellation *Made in NDC, Canada*. Shoddy-looking counterfeits from Asia and Germany flooded the market, but discerning buyers could tell the difference at the first whiff of Boredom: Not only did the Notre-Dame-du-Cachalot product calm even the most ardent desires, it left behind not the slightest aftertaste of regret. And so people worldwide shelled out exorbitant sums for a liquid that had been discovered quite by chance one fall day in 1971, in the backyard of a man called Caplan, or possibly Gaplan. Reserves were stockpiled everywhere. In teaching and literature departments the world over, inordinate—dare we say, dangerous—amounts were used. Television networks were also fond of the stuff. Publishers would use it to anoint their books, which would give off the scent for at least the first fifty readings. It even found its way into beer, cookies, cat food, and certain street drugs. As one columnist put it in *Cosmopolitan*: "Simply spritz yourself a cloud, immerse yourself in it, and soak it up."

Boredom was chic. Although too much of it could be lethal.

The people of Notre-Dame-du-Cachalot might well have become rich on the back of this discovery. They might have amassed Alberta-sized fortunes, had they been smart enough to control every stage of production. But unfortunately for them, Mayor Duressac had signed a nine hundred and ninety-nine year lease with the Yank, granting exclusive access to what appeared to be an unlimited supply of the stuff to Boston Boredom Inc. The village by the sea would of course enjoy a few trifling spinoffs and royalties generated by the meager salaries paid to the twenty-odd employees who saw to it that the pipes didn't leak and who filled the holds of the Liberian ships that transported the precious poison to other climes. Truth be told, the discovery had brought the villagers no end of new problems. The product in question, as everyone knows, must be used carefully, and administered at exactly the right dose. Countless accidental deaths were racked up each year in places that were too liberal with the liquid. It's all too easy to imagine how an entire village might slide into a deep depression that more often than not ended in suicide. Despite an abundance of caution, minor leaks were an everyday occurrence, and the village couldn't simply rely on the wind to cleanse the air. After all, on some summer days, the wind would die down completely or blow less hard than usual. Days like those ended with more fatalities. The victims would often be found standing up, their still-open eyes desperately seeking some diversion in the flight of a seabird, a strand of drool hanging from the corners of their mouths after they'd breathed their last.

And so, slowly but surely, the Ministry of GLUM's secret project neared its end. By the year 2000, the population of Notre-Dame-du-Cachalot had levelled off at 2,200 inhabitants. Not one of them considered leaving. Life in the village wasn't unpleasant. In fact, had it not been for the wind that continued to blow with all its might, life there would have been close to ideal. But on one peaceful evening in August 2000, the unthinkable happened: the wind stopped blowing over the Gaspé Peninsula, just as there sprung a leak in one of the pipes connected to the source of Boredom. For thirteen minutes, noxious fumes drifted from the geyser, mixing with the air in the sleeping village, and slipping inside Terese's open bedroom window. She was found dead as a doornail the next morning, the sole victim of a mini Bhopal. A favourite text from Marx still lay in her lap, open at a line that had been underlined in red. It was a text that she liked to turn to at times of uncertainty, and a line that she would often repeat to herself devoutly:

"Hegel remarks somewhere that all facts and personages of great importance in world history occur, as it were, twice. He forgot to add: the first time as tragedy, the second as farce."

Rosa had never fully understood what he meant by this, even though it succinctly summarized the path she was about to embark on. So the great minds who had met a tragic end were able to reincarnate themselves and come back to wander the earth as characters in a monumental farce? What a thought! Caesar, Louis XVI, and Dalida were going to reappear in some ridiculous form? It was something to ponder.

Zenaida made the macabre discovery. The village organized a funeral. Instead of flowers, red starfish, caught that same morning, were laid on her grave. It was Mayor Duressac who came up with the idea, having assisted Terese in her work as a trade unionist up until 1980. It was to him that the honour fell of wrapping his old comrade in the red flag and singing "Somewhere beyond the sea..." to her one last time. All the villagers, without exception, lined up to file past the casket. It was like a scene straight from Red Square at its pomp. The Ministry of GLUM even dispatched the ever-willing Madeleine Saint-Trombone to lay a wreath on Terese's casket along with a message of condolence signed in triplicate by the assistant deputy minister.

"Such a shame she left us in August, when she was so fond of lilaggs," Duressac sighed as he closed the casket, the last to gaze on the face of the dearly departed. Rosa insisted on burying her mother herself. "It's how things should be. I ggouldn't bear it if it were the other way round," she insisted, determined, as was only natural, to witness with her own eyes the loss that would leave her an orphan forever.

The other villagers were spared thanks only to an obsession with always closing their windows, for fear

that a sudden gust might sweep all their worldly possessions out to sea. But the August lull persisted. A cleansing
wind would not be coming. People began to die left, right,
and centre. By mid-August, a deathly calm reigned over
the village and folks holed up in their wooden homes,
afraid they would drop dead if they went about their
business outside. Notre-Dame-du-Cachalot had been
transformed into a huge gas chamber, strewn with dead
gulls and terns that had been struck down mid-flight,
betrayed by their instinct. The place was a wasteland.

Rosa had come to understand, ever since the Scrabble
prophecy, that she was the chosen one. And yet the
prophecy still needed some piecing together. It's one
thing to believe one is destined to accomplish great
things, but it's another thing altogether to be able to distinguish a "great thing" from a waste of time. Once again,
the answer came from the water. The following Saturday
afternoon, she ventured out onto the shore at low tide in
search of a sign of the west wind. The shore remained
the only place where the outside air was still breathable.
Ironically enough, it was during such bouts of solitary
introspection that the altruism she had inherited from
her mother inhabited her most fully. She knew that her
self-sacrifice was only a matter of time. But what form
would it take, what suffering would it relieve?

She chipped away at *A Contribution to the Critique
of Political Economy* and its tremendous chapter on precious metals—a passage that had in the past brought her
comfort since she could still hear her mother reading
her to sleep with it, on nights when the mournful howl-

ing of the wind prevented her from drifting off—but she could find no peace. There are voices in this world whose gentleness can heal all wounds. Crystal-clear tone, as anyone will tell you, imparts a certain richness and depth to even the most prosaic chants of workers and strikers, restoring to those unpopular texts the lustre of poetry with which they had been penned. Terese Ost's voice reading "The Precious Metals" came back to Rosa the way lullabies do to others. "They appear, so to speak, as solidified light raised from a subterranean world, since all the rays of light in their original composition are reflected by silver, while red alone, the colour of the highest potency, is reflected by gold." The memory of Terese's voice seemed to accompany the murmuring of the waves (or was it the sound of four million shrimp swallowing their food?) on a shimmering August afternoon. "The colour of the highest potency," she sobbed, falling into a kind of ideological trance that was closer to mysticism than to dialectics. She was wading through a frozen puddle of kelp when she spotted a huge winkle shell, its spiral as big as a human head. She'd never seen the like of it. In a childlike gesture, she brought the opening of the oversized winkle to her ear, listening for the sea. The sound that reached her left her rooted to the spot. The voice, *that* voice, the mother of all voices whispered to her from the depths of the shell: "Montreal. The wind comes from Montreal. That is where you will commit the unspeakable in order to save your village."

Prophecies are said to *come true*, an active form of verb that is not lost on us. Any prophecy, even one said

37

in jest after a heavy night's drinking, will set out to come true. We know this better than Rosa does. We're all too familiar with the macabre game of prophecies that announce themselves and set about coming true. Anyone boasting of *making* a prophecy come true is committing a pathetic act of blasphemy, setting themselves up for ridicule and obscurity.

Rosa had no more to her name than the five hundred dollars her mother had left her, a Scrabble set, a huge whelk that served as an oracle, and the chutzpah of youth that allows young people to simply up and leave one morning for Japan, convinced that everything will work out for the best, that things will be different for them. Old Zenaida found Rosa's departure harder to bear than Terese's sudden death. The prospect of finding herself alone in the village didn't appeal. The frail, arthritic creature clung to Rosa's shoulder, but the young girl had no desire for painful goodbyes. Distraught with sorrow, Zenaida fired off one proverb after the next, as though wanting to arm Rosa for her travels. "A rolling stone gathers no moss!" "Youth must have its fling!" Then, in one long sob as Rosa freed herself from her embrace and began to walk away, wracked with pain she called, "While the cat's away, the mice will blame their tools! Let a bird in the hand lie! A fool and his money speak louder than words! All roads lead to a journey of a thousand miles! A starving man is worth two in the bush!" If, at that very second, Rosa had looked back and seen the heap of wrinkles and grief dissolve into tears, she wouldn't have found the strength to leave. Her own cruelty would have turned her stomach. The old woman summoned the last of her strength to climb the stairs and collapse onto Rosa's bed, taking refuge in the girl's familiar smell and sinking into madness.

The villagers had spared Rosa until then for the sake of her mother, for whom they still had a little respect. Now alone with Aunt Zenaida, she had been reduced to nothing and risked becoming the fourth sister before long, or meeting the same fate as Terese had. She threw a few things into a bag and, using a purple knit sweater as a makeshift gas mask lest she come across the deadly fumes, took to the road that led to Route 132. She was ruined, orphaned, and bitter, but now she had a mission in life.

The unspeakable had better watch out.

::

Right at the entrance to Notre-Dame-du-Cachalot, a bridge spans the Massacre River, a trickle of water that's more strait than river and that owes its name to a bloody eighteenth-century skirmish between French settlers and the First Nations. Although most modern-day historians are quick to dismiss the story as legend, locals maintain that it was on that very spot that a band of warriors attacked, scalped, raped, burned, and pillaged (not necessarily in that order) twenty-two villagers whose only destiny had been that preordained by God. Today, a covered wooden bridge stands there, its oxblood-red colour, again according to legend, irrefutable proof of that act of barbarism. Even the gentle cooing of the turtledoves nesting in the rafters can't dispel the whiff of ill fortune that lingers over the place. A gaunt-faced man stands guard day and night at the far end of the picture-postcard bridge. He leans against the wooden railing and grabs for the camera that hangs around his neck any time a vehicle makes its way onto the creaking structure. Click. Everyone is immortalized. The handful of lost travellers furrow their brows at the ill-mannered oaf, but they don't dare strike up a conversation since one quick glance makes it abundantly clear that he's a simpleton. The twisted grin, the worn clothes, the dishevelled grey hair, the scar on the forehead... embarrassed at having stared at a lunatic for so long, the visitors avert their gaze from such unmistakable insanity. The village Cerberus films every single coming and going across the covered bridge. He leaves his post only to obey the most fundamental calls of nature, and sleeps no more than four hours a night. He'll see you crossing the bridge over the Massacre River; he'll see you, and your face will be added to the endless collection of mugshots in his modest, green-shingled home that stands at the entrance to the village.

Even to a local ear, the guardian's accent reverberates like an echo of yesteryear. He'd once been a mailman, a man of absolutely normal intelligence, making his rounds by bicycle. He'd delivered the rare mail that arrived from the outside world, right up until the day in May 1980 when a speeding car bearing plates from an English-speaking province knocked him flat on his back. The culprit—doubtless one of the owners of the soon-to-be-shuttered pulp and paper mill—sped off, never to be found. The mailman spent months in bed, his faculties irreversibly affected, his mind now filled only with the image of a fair-haired man at the wheel of an enormous car that had sent him flying into a ditch. Ever since, his life had been nothing but one long tale of woe. Unable to take to his bicycle again, he was reduced to getting by on a paltry post office pension. On cold winter nights, the pain from his arthritis, another consequence of the accident, would leave him wishing he were dead. There he would stand, waiting in vain for the reckless driver to cross his path again so that he could take his photo. This (to his mind) irrefutable evidence of the attack he'd suffered all those years earlier would see justice prevail. Napoleon—that was his name—was out for retribution. And so, as she crossed the wooden bridge, Rosa heard the camera go "click" as Napoleon snapped a photo of the young girl's silhouette, framed by the covered bridge. And so it was that Rosa's final moment in the village she was leaving behind forever was captured on the film of a madman who just wouldn't let go of a grudge. The picture would join those of hundreds of other silhouettes of boys and girls who had one day packed up all their worldly possessions and left Notre-Dame-du-Cachalot for life in the city. Without a word to anyone, Napoleon would pin up their photos on the wall of his home. None were recognizable, each standing in the shadows, their backs to the camera, not even aware they'd had their picture taken. No smiles, not so much as a wave good-bye, not a tear, nothing but departures by the hundred. Silhouettes of a rural exodus.

Having recognized young Rosa, Napoleon legged it over to the town hall to let Mayor Duressac know. The village had allowed a good number of its inhabitants to slip away after the plant had closed, but this was too much. How many times had Napoleon heard the mayor say, "Where would we be without Terese?" And now the person who most closely resembled the late trade unionist was slinking away from Notre-Dame-du-Cachalot. The mailman took it to be further proof of the curse that afflicted the village. He hammered breathlessly on Duressac's door. No reply. He went around the back of the house, where he found the mayor, nose and mouth protected against deathly Boredom by a surgical mask, busily scrubbing a large bowl of mussels. From time to time, the elected official would look up to toss a broken mussel down onto the pebbles on the shore.

"What're you gglammoring about, Napoleon?"

"It's young Rosa Ost! She's turning her bagg on her native village! Why is she being allowed to leave?"

"I know, my friend. I know. She's off to Montreal."

"Montreal? Is she ggrazy? It's way too big for a little girl. She's gonna get lost. She'll get eaten alive."

Napoleon held his head in his hands.

"She's off to find the wind. The others are dropping ligge flies. A shellfish told her. A winggle, by all aggounts."

"Winggles ggan be wrong. More often than not, they're all talgg... It's very brave of her, all the same. But she's so young, so innocent. Do you thingg she'll magg it? I'm sure she will!"

42

"I don't know, Napoleon. She's our last chance. If you asgg me, I thingg we've seen the last of her. She won't be ggoming bagg."

"Why not, Mayor Duressagg? Why won't she be bagg?"

"Have you seen many young girls ligge Rosa ggome bagg from Montreal? They leave and they don't ggome bagg. As for the wind, let's just say I'm a little sggeptiggal."

"But what if she pulls it off? Won't she be the living proof for her late mother that you ggan change the world by having a child?"

"I should've seen that ggoming from you. Ggome off it, Napoleon!"

"Just thingg about it, Mr. Mayor. If Rosa manages to whip up the west wind and save her village, it will be a fine tribute to her mother's memory. Don't you remember that poor woman lived her whole life for other people?"

"And loogg where that got her! Just remember what ggarried her off."

"Well, if Rosa succeeds, then she'll be avenged."

"I'm not so sure, Napoleon. Things are much more 'komplikated' in the city, as they say. She'll end up meeting all gginds of weirdos. She'll lose sight of her mission in no time."

Napoleon was smiling now.

"I'm sure she'll manage it. Terese was ligge those mussels you're sggrubbing. They lay their eggs wherever the ggurrent ggarries them. They never get to see their children grow up. They drift off to ggongger their eggosystem. Their offspring turn the world blue, the very ggolour it needs."

"And that's what's giving you hope, Napoleon?"

"Of ggourse it is! The way she goes about her life gives her every hope. No matter how things turn out, she'll know she was useful, just ligge her mother."

"And that didn't get poor Terese very far."

"Thingg about it, Mayor Duressagg. If Rosa suggseeds, Terese's memory will be honoured, and some of the glory will refleggt bagg on us."

"I thingg we should be more ligge sea gulls, ligge that one over there. They don't spend their whole lives moping around in the same spot. They're always on the move, and they tagge ggare of their young. They don't let them leave the nest. And if they do, then they're banished for life. If they run off and dare to ggome bagg, their parents swallow them whole!"

"That's horrible!"

"That's how it is with birds. Ggome on, Napoleon. Don't worry about young Rosa. She'll ggome running bagg in no time."

The former mailman trudged back to his post. At the other end of the bridge, where the paved road of civilization picked up again, stood a board two metres high by three metres wide that the mayor and Terese Ost had put up a long, long time ago on the orders of the Ministry of GLUM. Weather-beaten white letters set against a faded green background spelled out to any literate traveller emerging from the darkness of the covered bridge the basic rules of conduct that had, with time, wind, and rain, lost a little more of their clarity with every passing year.

SIX DIRECTIVES FOR THE INTENTION
OF CITIZENS WHO ABANDON
NOTRE-DAME-DU-CACHALOT

1. If you are travelling to Montreal, GLUM strongly recommends you dress in keeping with the style of the times, so as to avoid disapproving looks when you reach the city.

2. You are entitled to keep your accent. However, you should be aware that beyond Sainte-Flavie, you will become part of an audible, ridiculous minority.

3. In the unlikely event of a return to your homeland, we would appreciate it if you would speak as little as possible of everything you ate, encountered, admired, learned, or enjoyed in the outside world.

4. Please rid yourself of all feelings of belonging, roll them carefully up into a ball, and throw them into the Massacre River, where they will become salmon bait.

5. Discretion is vital when you are asked where you come from. We recommend that you claim to be from Cap-Chat, Baie-des-Oursins, or Matane.

6. Understand that upon leaving the paradise in which GLUM generously allowed you to be born, you hereby renounce all possibility of returning home without being subjected to opprobrium and ill will.

ENJOY YOUR TRIP!

"Duly noted," Rosa said to herself.

By the side of Route 132, as the fine rain misted down, she joined a group of young, outrageously made-up strippers who, like her, were looking for a way to get to the city. The exotic dancers had been travelling from one Gaspé community to the next, performing, in squalid smoke-filled venues, dance routines that were to eroticism what the hot dog is to gastronomy. With tawdry taste and a distinct lack of subtlety, they migrated along Route 132 like egrets in their breeding plumage. Each of the showgirls spoke with an accent that charmed Rosa. They'd just been dropped off the day after a show in a none-too-savoury bar in Gaspé. They weren't displeased at the prospect of returning to Montreal. A girl called Jasmine, who seemed to be the group's leader, handed Rosa a flyer for the routine they'd been performing across the province since June. The poetry of the names struck a chord with Rosa. "This evening's dazzling troupe consists of a group of independent young women under the direction of Jasmine Bérubé. The dance routines performed for your pleasure by Tatiana and Ludmilla (Saint Petersburg), Carlota and Roberta (Santiago de Cuba), Shu-Misty (People's Republic of China), Blondie and Nelly (Leipzig, ex-GDR), and the stunning Mimi and Suzie (Mozambique and Angola) will guarantee you sleepless nights for years to come..."

Huddled inside the deserted bus stop, the noisy crowd fell silent when the newcomer appeared. Rosa looked like a nun next to the flamboyant flock of dancers. Wearing a lilac dress that would have been the height of fashion in 1912, she found herself surrounded by leather miniskirts, vertiginous stiletto heels, and gaudily made-up faces. We couldn't say for sure what sparked the snickering that greeted her arrival. Fingers could definitely be pointed at the pre-First World War outfit or the russet country-girl hairstyle, or maybe it was the face bereft of makeup, a face that was neither ugly nor pretty, a face eroded by years of salty air. We've all known these children from the middle of nowhere, their rural tics, that way they have of staring at you, their odd habit of talking to every stranger as though they're chatting to their brother. They're all over our cities. They speak in sepia and stare after the ambulances we've long since stopped hearing. Rosa is their queen.

Ha! ha! ha!

What a hick!

Straight from the sticks!

She's come down from the mountains!

She's left her rolling prairies!

With all the grace of a walrus on an ice floe!

Wearing a filthy hand-knit scarf!

This is her body, escaped the back of beyond, given up for us!

I bet it takes her twenty years to tone down her accent, then another twenty trying to get it back.

The strippers were loving it. She made an easy target.

Jasmine told her that the group had been waiting for over two hours for a bus to bring them back to civilization. They were running low on smokes, and growing impatient. "Who the hell do they think they are, for crap's sake!" a platinum blonde kept whining, crushing every cigarette butt she could find beneath her heel to pass the time. .

Just as they had resigned themselves to hitching a lift, a minivan came around the corner, a young man at the wheel. The minivan pulled up in front of the shelter, and the driver stepped out slowly. What they had all thought from a distance to be a skinny, long-haired boy in his teens turned out to be a woman who was at least half a century old. It was an easy mistake to make. Clearly, the ambivalence was carefully curated. Curiously enough, the showgirls were lost for words. Rosa, who was used to seeing boyish-looking girls at the Marxist talks her mother had often taken her to, piped up.

"Did you see a bus behind you?"

"No bus today. It's Saturday."

"Ah! Oggay."

"But I can always drop yizall somewhere."

"We're all headed for Montreal. If you ggould tagge us as far as Rimousggui, that would sure help us out."

The Amazon burst out laughing.

"Rimousggui? You sure talgg ligge you're from around here, dontcha?" she teased.

"Uh, yes, I do. My name's Rosa Ost. I'm from Notre-Dame-du-Ggachalot, just on the other side of the ggovered bridge."

"Well, *I'm* Jeanne Joyal. Hop in. It's freezing out here. What a friggin' freeze-your-butt-off country we live in. Just one thing—I'll take y'all to Montreal, cos that's where I'm headed. But I don't wanna hear one single cuss word outta you, and I don't wanna smell one single cigarette in my van. If I do, you won't be long for this world. Deal?"

48

Jeanne Joyal's "*I'm*" came out deep and strong as she pounded her right index finger into her chest, as though afraid someone might mistake who was talking. It resonated in the air like a despairing bellow, an order, a threat. No swearing, then. Though she wasn't exactly elegance and grace personified herself... The girls decided not to point out the irony, afraid that might spell an end to any hopes of a lift. The dancers didn't have a choice. Either they agreed to the deal or they'd freeze to death by the side of the road out in the middle of nowhere. There was nothing else for it. They all squeezed into the van, repressing their nicotine cravings for hours, and kept quiet, not trusting themselves to stick to the rules. After all, cussing is second nature to strippers. Rosa sat next to Jeanne, who for the first three hours of a trip that would take them ten, withdrew into impenetrable silence. Huddled together in the back of the van, the other women did what everyone does when they wind up someplace warm after spending hours freezing by the roadside: they fell asleep. The ten entangled dancers formed a single dozing mass of bodies, faces, and earrings. Rosa stared at the heap in the rearview mirror until sleep got the better of the misgivings she felt about Jeanne Joyal. She dreamt of a sailboat, a departure, a king who no longer knew what to do with his daughters.

"Where am I?"

A road riddled with potholes. A yellow line that was always double. To her right, the St. Lawrence River: slack, huge, swollen, and extravagant. To her left, the hostile forest: mysterious, crackling, and dense. Saint-

Ulric, Baie-des-Sables, Les Boules, Métis-sur-Mer, Sainte-Flavie... Rosa wondered what pathetic, imperialist reactionary moron had come up with the bright idea of naming his village Les Boules. Was there a town anywhere else in Canada called Boobies? She squinted and saw the north shore of the St. Lawrence for the first time in her life, fighting back the urge to shout, "Land ahoy!"

It wasn't until they reached Rimouski that Jeanne struck up a conversation.

"Bit of a hole, isn't it, Notre-Dame-du-Cachalot?"

"Pardon me?"

"Your village. Bit of a backwoods, innit?"

"It has its charms."

How wonderful to see the little Gaspé girl fend off the strippers' gibes and Jeanne Joyal's insults. Was it down to stoicism? Upbringing? Naivety? In fact, it's a winning blend of all three that allows anyone leaving the Gaspé Peninsula to survive contact with other Quebecers. Thousands of kilometres away, Tyroleans receive the same blessings from birth, preparing them to withstand the sneers from Vienna. That's just how things are. You mustn't think the insults just slid off Rosa's woollen scarf like water off a duck's back. They fell into a well as deep as Percé Rock is long. One day, the well would suddenly erupt with insults that had been fermenting there for years, and the poor man or woman who delivered the final insult would end up with putrid egg on their face. It turns out that someone was once given a pile of money to come up with a name for this phenomenon. They called it *transfer*. Fortunately for Jeanne Joyal, Rosa's well was still virtually empty.

The news that Jeanne passed on to Rosa was as valuable as it was worrying. For months, Montreal had been in the grip of a housing crisis of unprecedented proportions. Finding somewhere affordable to live had become practically impossible. The newspapers were full of classified ads of people looking for a room to share. Some would stop at nothing to get what they were looking for. Rosa could see that for herself as she leafed through a newspaper that was lying in the glove compartment. "Young professional man, 26, handsome, muscular, quiet, fond of cooking and cleaning, looking for room to rent asap." "Curvaceous student, 18, calm and quiet, looking for affordable room." "Single woman looking for apartment to share. Open to anything. *Anything*." For a moment, Rosa imagined herself sleeping on a park bench, shivering as passersby gaped on their way past.

"You headed there for school?"

"No, I wish, but I have an important mission to aggomplish. What about you? What brought you to the Gaspé Peninsula? You talgg ligge you're from Montreal."

Jeanne burst out laughing. "Listen, Rosa, it's not my problem, but you're the one going to Montreal. I'd start making a big effort to pronounce my Ks, if I were you. If you don't, people are gonna start thinking you're not the sharpest tool in the box! Just some friendly advice."

"Do you really thingg people'll notice?"

Belly laugh.

"Oggey-doggey." She screwed up her face. "It feels like I'm swallowing sand. Okey-dokey. Phew! OK, so what brought you to the Gaspé Peninsula?"

"Vacation in Percé."

"At the end of August? Wasn't it a little chilly?"

"Yeah, but it was cheaper."

"And what do you do in Montreal?"

"I work part-time at the Office québécois de la langue française."

"Oh! You're a terminologist?"

"Jeez no! That'd bore me to tears. I'm a Frenchification officer for small businesses."

"And what does that involve?"

"I roam around in my truck looking for posters written in English or Chinese all across Montreal. When I find one, I report the business to my superiors."

"Ooh. And what happens then?"

"That's none of my business. I do my job, then they do theirs. So, what's your mission, then?"

"I have to get the west wind up and blowing again. It's urgent."

Jeanne Joyal beat her forehead three times against the steering wheel.

"Wow! The west wind, eh? So, what's 'the west wind' shorthand for back in good old NDC?"

"It means just that: 'the west wind.' My village will be wiped off the face of the earth if I don't succeed."

Her tongue running away with her as the showgirls snored in the back, Rosa told Jeanne all about Notre-Dame-du-Cachalot's sad fate. She spared no detail, making an effort to leave no K unpronounced. She even produced the oracle/winkle from her bag, but it wouldn't speak. Jeanne Joyal listened to her passenger without saying a word. By the time the story was finished, the van was already past Longueuil. Their trip, Rosa's story, and Jeanne Joyal's patience were on the final straight. A few of the girls had woken up and begun biting their nails, although there was no way to tell if that was down to lack of nicotine or because they were captivated by Rosa's story. Jasmine, normally the least focused of all the group, couldn't have been more engrossed in the story if it had been a 1950s radio soap opera. Completely caught up in the winkle's prophecy, she forgot all about Jeanne Joyal's ban and, as though propelled by an unstoppable force, lit up a Du Maurier Extra Light just as the story ended. Jeanne Joyal saw the flicker of the lighter's flame in the rearview mirror and tightened her grip on the steering wheel. A look of terror crossed her face, although only Rosa glimpsed her panicked expression, catching the flame's reflection in Jeanne's dilated pupils. Could it be that she was travelling with a pyrophobe?

The first puff on a cigarette after a good story well told. "Aaahh," Jasmine sighed.

It has to be said that Rosa knew how to tell a good story. Another natural tendency. And it wasn't uncommon to see fans of good stories light up a smoke whenever Rosa finished one of her tales. So can Rosa really be blamed for the drama that was about to unfold as the acrid smoke from Jasmine's cigarette wafted into Jeanne Joyal's nostrils? Should fate really have to explain why Jeanne picked up on that very same smoke just as the van was crossing the Jacques Cartier Bridge?

"Why you little—" Jeanne screamed.

The brake hit the floor. The van's doors were flung open. "Out!" Jeanne Joyal had blocked the traffic on the bridge and already the first movement of a symphony of car horns could be heard. The strippers filed out of the vehicle, without so much as a glance at the woman who had given them a lift. The car horns blared even louder. The silhouettes of ten exotic dancers slowly made their way across the Montreal skyline. To the left of the illuminated cross on Mount Royal went Suzie, Mimi, Blondie, Shu-Misty, and Nelly. To the right shuffled Roberta, the Saint Petersburg twins Ludmilla and Tatiana, and Carlota and Jasmine. The van now contained only Jeanne Joyal, Rosa Ost, a lime-coloured false nail, a tube of mascara, and stony silence.

"That'll show 'em! That's the only language people like that understand, I'm tellin' you. Where do they get it from, eh? Give 'em an inch and they take a mile!"

Without knowing why, Rosa slipped the tube of mascara into her bag. Even though the punishment seemed a little harsh to her, her admiration for Jeanne at that moment knew no bounds. At last, a real leader! At last, a woman who had the courage of her convictions, who stuck to her guns. The girls had been warned; they'd known what they'd signed up for. Rosa couldn't help but draw a parallel between the inveterate smoker and the men and women who had betrayed the revolution. The common good had to prevail. Since the prophecy had been revealed, propelling her out into the world, the young woman had almost stopped believing in chance. When it came down to it, she thought to herself, the unexpected encounter with Jeanne Joyal was more like an appointment than a coincidence. By the time they reached the city centre, Jeanne had calmed down and confessed to Rosa that she wasn't sure what to make of the whole west wind thing. Rosa was going to have her work cut out, she told her. Montrealers didn't have much time for the wind. She also told Rosa that she happened to own a boarding house in the Villeray neighbourhood, just north of the Jean-Talon market. She'd been careful not to mention it in front of the strippers for fear she would have to turn them away for being too rough around the edges, which would have gone against the Housing Board's laws. But Rosa was welcome to stay. The room would cost her five hundred dollars a month, and that included breakfast and supper, two balanced meals that Jeanne prepared herself, drawing on *Canada's Food Guide* and *Enjoying the Art of Canadian Cooking* by Jehane Benoît. Rosa learned that several other young women roomed at Jeanne's house, too, and that there reigned in the Villeray home a spirit of friendship and camaraderie. Each lodger was expected to help with the housework, which made perfect sense to Rosa. She liked the idea, although she wasn't sure if she'd be able to stay for very long. She expected to find an answer to the challenge set by the winkle quite quickly, and couldn't commit to spending more than a month in Montreal. Her landlady-to-be reassured her: unlike the other girls, Rosa wouldn't have to sign a lease or even make a verbal agreement. She could stay as long as she liked.

For a moment, Rosa imagined that Lady Luck was on her side. Although she had only five hundred dollars, barely enough to cover one month at Jeanne's. She would need a job. And Jeanne was less reassuring when it came to finding work. There were few options in Montreal for a young girl with no qualifications, no matter how well read she was. The job market was looking for people with skills. What could Rosa do? Very little, when it came down to it. Rosa pored over the classified ads in a newspaper she found under the seat. All the job openings were for everything she was not: bilingual, a visible minority, with five years of experience, etc. But just before being expelled from the van, a long Germanic hand sporting false orange nails had pressed a newspaper cutting into Rosa's palm. Rosa silently thanked Nelly.

NIGHT RECEPTIONIST at downtown hotel. Excellent communication + basic accountancy skills required. Bilingualism a plus. Inquire for details at the Butler Motor Hotel. 1199 blvd Saint-Laurent, Montreal.

The ad seemed to have been written just for Rosa. Sure, it was a stretch to call herself bilingual, but she'd manage. "Practice makes perfect," she thought to herself. Deciding to try her luck, Rosa asked Jeanne to drop her off at the address in the ad. When Rosa asked what she thought her chances were of finding the wind in Montreal, Jeanne told her that it was certainly possible. In a world where everything from cleanliness to godliness could be bought and sold, she said, it was entirely possible that the wind had become a commodity, too.

56

First the van pulled up outside McGill University on Sherbrooke. The city was so bright, Rosa hardly knew which way to turn. Three horse-faced students crossed the street as Rosa looked on in astonishment. They were anemic blond, their oversized teeth cutting a path before them, dressed in colours fit for a funeral, their laughter constant and shrill. It was the laughter of the money-grubber, of those so caught up in a world of lavish lifestyles and allowances that they couldn't bear to be ignored. It seemed to Rosa that it was the kind of laugh you could never learn; they'd been born with it.

"Anglos!" Jeanne remarked. "They're so friggin' ugly."

Then came the litter-strewn streets and the parks where the homeless pitched their tents.

"Alrighty, girl. I've gotta leave you here. Here's my address and phone number. If ever you get into trouble, just gimme a call. Good luck with your interview."

Rosa didn't know how to thank the woman who'd driven her more than a thousand kilometres without asking for a cent, who'd listened to her country bumpkin stories, and who was now offering her room and board. It was like Jeanne Joyal was made of the very same steel that was used to forge the liberating swords of the oppressed. Before dropping Rosa outside an Agatha Christie-esque stone building, Jeanne told her that this was Boulevard Saint-Laurent and that she should be careful: it wasn't the safest part of town. She should take the number 55 bus straight to Villeray after the interview.

CHAPTER 2

Night on the Nile

WE SEE HER ALONE, standing in front of a huge greystone building, more than a thousand kilometres from home, with nothing other than a small backpack. Let's take a moment to shed a tear over little Rosa's fate. She would have given her very soul for Jeanne Joyal—for whom her admiration had grown out of all proportion over the course of a few short hours—to bring her straight home to her village. Boulevard Saint-Laurent loomed before her like a wound. She was used to the calm of the countryside, and her eyes struggled to take in everything happening around her. Her senses were bombarded from all sides. Outside the Montreal Pool Room, a human wreck who was screaming that the end of the world was nigh was being dragged off by men in white coats armed with syringes. A blonde African woman cheeped into her phone, wagging a finger in the air. *Phoque* this and *phoque* that, something about seals.

Rosa made her way nervously into the hotel. At the far end of the left side of the lobby was a staircase that led up to the rooms. The front desk was to her right. Behind it, there was a mirror and a door that no doubt led to a small office. Rosa could make out a purring voice. Schmaltzy music dripped from a speaker on the wall. The room smelled of mould and curry. Rosa put down her backpack and pressed timidly on the bell. An Indian man emerged from the office, dabbing at his mouth with a napkin.

"Yes. I'm sorry, I was eating."

The man chewed slowly on the last morsel of what must have been a specialty from his homeland. Rosa's belly rumbled. She had never smelled fresh curry before. Every molecule in her digestive system begged her to ask if she could try some, but her manners won the day.

"I'm... My name's Rosa Ost. I'm here about the ad."

Rosa set the scrap of newspaper down on the counter.

"You speak English?" the man asked in a sing-song voice.

"Yes."

"You've done this before?"

"Err, yes... in Percé... in Gaspésie," she lied.

The man's eyes widened at the sound of the word *Gaspésie*. He launched into a monologue that was more opera than speech. Rosa was fairly certain he was describing how he'd spent his vacation there in the company of a charming woman. She'd played her cards right, by the

60

looks of things. His eyes moist, he waxed lyrical about how beautiful the peninsula was, how welcoming its people were, how wonderful it had been to admire the colony of gannets on Bonaventure Island. To make sure she understood, he began strutting like a bird behind the counter, squawking loudly. Then he stretched his arms out as if to take flight. He produced a two-year-old calendar from a drawer and showed Rosa pictures of Percé Rock, the cliffs at Forillon, a fishing boat, and other photos of the region. Rosa came to understand that another Gaspé girl before her had ensured that the man from India, his voice now trembling with emotion, would welcome her with open arms. She also realized that she had just put her foot in it by saying that she spoke English. It just so happened that the woman with whom he had spent his vacation in Percé back in 1989 had cast such a spell over him that he had been left fascinated by, and nostalgic for, all things French. Rosa was glad that the mysterious lover hadn't taken her man to see the mountains of Charlevoix instead.

"Do you know how to do the books?"

Rosa thought for a moment. It would be untruthful to say yes. She *did* know how to work out the value-form using the Marxist formula. She had also read about the difference between assets and liabilities, and that the two had to balance, but it would have been a stretch to expect a salary in return for this knowledge. She wondered what she should say. More than anything, she had to start looking for the wind just as soon as she could. This job was just a way to pay the bills while she went about her real work. And so she told the lie that would pay the rent.

"Yes," she told the man.

"Good! I'm Sri Satyanarayana. When can you start?"

"Tomorrow, if you like, Mr. Satyanarayana."

He grinned. He still couldn't believe that such a naïve young girl had shown up at his door just like that, ready to do an ill-paid job that nobody else wanted. The few other candidates who had come had turned their noses up at the salary on offer. The place didn't exactly inspire confidence. It felt safe enough so long as people were still walking by outside, but in the dark of night, the Butler Motor Hotel was nothing short of grim. He secretly thanked Vishnu for having sent him this Gaspé girl. She reminded him of happy times, laughed at his gannet impression, and was polite. Even more extraordinary, she called him Mr. Satyanarayana—for the first time in his life he'd met a Quebecer who could pronounce his name correctly. Sri Satyanarayana had been sharing the three hotel shifts with his younger brother for the past two months, and he was fed up. The girl was a godsend, and he decided to hire her on the spot. In the hours that followed, Rosa was transformed from an idle villager into an active member of the workforce. As Sri explained the record books, the rooms, the spreadsheets, and the schedules for the cleaning staff, she could feel welling up inside her the sense of importance that prompts so many young people to trade the best years of their life for a pittance of a salary. Sri explained that, despite the hotel's reputation for being a hovel, it welcomed all kinds of celebrities, from singers and politicians to judges and journalists. There was even a well-known dance troupe

62

that often stayed there, but he couldn't name names. Rosa promised to respect the anonymity of all those who appeared before her counter. She would be working alone all night and, as well as renting out the rooms, would have to keep an eye on the hotel's accounts and balance the books each morning. Sri spoke very quickly and with an Indian accent, causing Rosa's head to spin as her long journey began to catch up with her.

After three hours of intense training, Rosa bade farewell to Sri Satyanarayana until the following evening at midnight. Giddy with hunger, her head full of numbers and instructions, she made her way south. Increasingly disturbing individuals wandered the sidewalks. And that's when it happened. A young man, pupils dilated, bumped into her and told her in no uncertain terms to watch where she was going. Another elbowed her out of the way. Each aggression added to the tiredness and hunger she felt, giving way to an entirely new phenomenon for our little Rosa. She didn't feel it coming, just like the captain of the *Titanic* didn't see the wretched iceberg. She was still cursing that rude young man. It was hardly worth mentioning, yet at the same time it was something immense and irreversible. The right half of Rosa's top lip rose ever so slightly, as though dragged upwards by an invisible, painless fish hook. The sneer lasted all of five seconds, the time it took her to breathe out, the time it took her to realize she'd just lost the teensiest bit of the control she'd always exercised over her nervous system. She paid very little attention to the incident. Too little. Those who knew her knew she hadn't inherited that strange tic from her mother. Terese Ost's placid features never flinched in the face of adversity. It wasn't a Gaspé sneer.

Rosa's last meal had been in Notre-Dame-du-Cachalot, and she looked around for somewhere to eat. It was her nose that led her across Boulevard René-Lévesque and into Chinatown, where she gazed longingly at the stalls of exotic fruit. Most of the restaurants were closed, apart from one that was playing a piece of music that she knew. Surely not! No, there was no mistaking it, that really was the *Internationale* she could hear coming from the little Vietnamese restaurant! "Arise, ye prisoners of starvation! Arise, ye wretched of the earth!" The revolutionary anthem ramped Rosa's hunger up a notch. Imagine her surprise when she walked into the dining room only to see her showgirl friends gathered around a long table, singing their hearts out as Ludmilla and Tatiana conducted the impromptu choir with their chopsticks. A waiter was busy bringing the performers their food. Rosa burst into tears of joy upon being reunited with her travelling companions.

"Suzie, Mimi, Blondie, Shu-Misty, Nelly! And Jasmine... I didn't think I'd ever see you again!"

After being cast out of Jeanne Joyal's van, the girls had marched all the way to Place des Arts, before heading over to the Butler Motor Hotel, where they usually stayed. Their adventures had left them hungry, and so they'd gone out in search of a good pho. They all kissed each other on the cheek. Two or three times on each cheek. It lasted a solid ten minutes, as the waiters looked on, exchanging smiles.

"Where did you learn the *Internationale*? Are you party members?"

Rosa couldn't believe it. She was fully aware of the ideological ocean that separated her from the rest of humanity, yet here were her comrades, in her hour of need. She felt like a Christian, alone on the sand of the Coliseum, as the wild beast prepared to enter the arena to devour her, exchanging words with a stranger who was also a believer. Jasmine brought her back down to earth.

"Party? No, no, it's just a song Ludmilla and Tatiana taught us for one of our routines. We wear old Red Army uniforms and peel them off one piece at a time to the music. We keep going until you can see *everything*. It's always a big hit. The audience laps it up."

Rosa couldn't help but find it a little blasphemous, even iconoclastic, to use the *Internationale* in that way, but she couldn't very well tear a strip off the only people she knew in Montreal besides Jeanne Joyal and Sri Satyanarayana.

"So, did you find the wind, little one?" Jasmine asked.

"No, not yet, but I found a job! It's just across the street at the Butler—"

The girls howled with approval.

"That's where we're staying! That's great! We'll see each other every night!" Ludmilla crowed, raising her cup of jasmine tea in a toast to their new alliance.

The rest of the evening went by in the typical calm, humid contentment of Montreal in August. Rosa learned how to say "I love you" in Russian, Spanish, German, and Chinese. Blondie and Nelly did their utmost to get her to pronounce *"ich"* the right way. The girls insisted that Rosa eat with them. Huge portions of noodle soup arrived, topped with mint leaves, green onions, and big strips of rare beef. As she eyed the blood-red flesh, Rosa couldn't help but think of Marx once again: "They appear, so to speak, as solidified light raised from a subterranean world, since all the rays of light in their original composition are reflected by silver, while red alone, the colour of the highest potency, is reflected by gold." *Raised from a subterranean world*, that's exactly how Rosa felt as that Saturday neared its end. She tipped the beef into the boiling broth with a poke of her chopstick. The redness disappeared as the meat cooked before her very eyes, and she gobbled up the soup hungrily.

It was the most exquisite meal of her life. And she would spend the rest of her days trying to repeat the experience.

::

Almost directly opposite the Butler Motor Hotel, where Boulevard Saint-Laurent brings new meaning to the word *sordid*, there stands a Montreal institution that has survived the stock market crash of 1929, the Great Depression, the second world war, the sixties, disco, Quebec's newfound internationalism, four PQ election wins, two referendums, and the very best efforts of Montreal's vice squad. Opened in 1925 by a Bessarabian immigrant named Epstein, it has changed hands six times and changed names three times, but its vocation has remained unchanged: a venue for the performing arts. Night on the Nile was an old-style cabaret with a picture-frame stage, the almost entirely male audience seated around it at large, rustic wooden tables. Sold in 1945 to an Italian by the name of Battista, the club was known until 1979 as *The Hairy Palm*, only to be renamed *La Paume hirsute* one year later to comply with Quebec's new language law, after the government consulted a group of freshly minted linguists from the Université de Montréal who debated for eight days before coming up with a new name for the temple to feminine beauty. After hours spent searching for equivalencies in the hopes of preserving the name's *otherness*, a search that came to an abrupt end the day the budget allocated to the operation ran dry, the purists had insisted on *Le Hairy Palm*, while the fanatics among them, driven by an abstruse nationalistic sentiment, insisted the venue be named *La souveraine beauté*, sovereign beauty. *La Paume hirsute* was a concession that never took hold, and the cabaret remained, to all Montrealers and to all visitors in search of a touch of the exotic, the good old Nile. It was on the stage of that smoke-filled cabaret that our group of strippers, known to one and all as Lenin's Great-Granddaughters, wowed audiences.

For five years, they had been performing the same well-oiled show, occasionally heading off to the Quebec countryside to leave the Montreal public wanting more, in no doubt that they would forever be able to count on a faithful and generous following in the city. The eighty-five-minute show was an erotic creation inspired by the Bolshevik Revolution that ran twice nightly from

Thursday to Sunday, even on statutory holidays (when the artists were paid double time under Quebec's labour standards law). By 10 p.m. any poor chump still harbouring hopes of finding a seat was out of luck. The place would already be crawling with college students, university types, singles, bar-hopping married men, soldiers on leave, the odd Conservative MP, and even, rumour had it, the upper echelons of the Ottawa police force. By 9:50 p.m. the feverish teens from the local college were already hammering on the tables, chanting "Le-nin! Le-nin! Le-nin!" in the vain hopes of seeing the curtain rise a little earlier than usual. But the strippers were as regular as a Swiss timepiece, taking orders only from their lead choreographer Jasmine, a bombshell who'd been born in Sept-Îles and raised in Gatineau, her body the cause of no end of insomnia from coast to coast over the years.

At ten o'clock sharp, the racket would become unbearable and the first fights would already be breaking out in the back corners of the hall. Everyone was after the same thing: an unobstructed view of the stage that promised to light up any second. The first cuss words rang out in D flat, in both official languages. Then suddenly the lights dimmed, bringing an end to the hoots and the whistles, just as it would have for a class of overexcited schoolchildren. A silence as thick as the ambient air fell over the room. Then a blue spotlight cast its cold glare over Tatiana, who was wearing a sable coat and a fur hat with a red star on the front. Squatting on an overturned wooden crate, she shivered in spite of her getup and the Dantean heat of the room. She was in full character. Backstage, Jasmine started up the soundtrack to the intoxicating spectacle. A sexy voice purred: "Ladies and gentlemen, please welcome Ludmilla and Tatiana..." The wind raced across the steppes, then the heart-rending notes of the balalaika launched into the opening bars of "Lara's Theme" from *Doctor Zhivago*. Now Ludmilla made her entrance, dressed as a Red Army soldier. She came up behind poor, trembling Tatiana, then plunged her slender socialist hands down inside her compatriot's fur collar, languidly stroking her skin until she stopped shivering. Uniform and fur coat gradually fell away, piece by piece, to the tune of the Red Army Choir playing *The Kossack's Song*. By that time, the number of dislocated jaws and souls condemned to eternal damnation were already beyond counting in the room. The two nymphs of Saint Petersburg, now completely naked, offered up a lascivious interpretation of *The Dying Swan* worthy of the Bolshoi. The Manitobans in the audience, who had driven all the way from Winnipeg, sobbed with desire. Then the two Russians, now glowing with perspiration, embraced passionately and left the stage, to the beat of *Ra Ra Rasputin*. A first burst of thunderous applause, followed by ape-like whoops of delight, followed them backstage.

"And now, direct from Leipzig, Germany, please welcome Blooooondie and Neeeeeelly!" Blondie and Nelly, two Nordic beauties who had been born during the heyday of the German Democratic Republic, their feminine charms left unaltered by the mysterious injections of their national swim team, entered stage left to Wagner's

Valkyries, bedecked in horned helmets and steel bikinis. "*Wunderbaaaaaar*," roared the crowd, eyes bulging. Buoyed by the warm welcome, the two Teutons shimmied and swayed provocatively to Nina Hagen's greatest hits in a display that left nothing to the imagination. The routine ended with a stroke of truly original and utterly Germanic inspiration with Blondie, stretched backwards over a hobby horse on wheels, squirting a tube of Leipzig mustard over her navel, and Nelly, a frankfurter clenched between her lips, dipping it into the mustard before bringing it to Blondie's mouth. Her eyes rolling back in her head, Blondie licked the sausage clean then devoured it, before Nelly climbed astride her partner and wheeled the horse offstage, the strange pair exiting in a burst of red light to Nina Hagen's rendering of *New York, New York*.

That Eurotrash fantasy was followed by a Shu-Misty solo. Shu-Misty's first name was actually just Shu. The Asian angel had entered Canada illegally, stowed away in a shipping container that was supposed to contain nothing but made-in-China shoes. The girl's grandmother had fallen victim to a hip fracture after slipping on an octopus left lying on the kitchen floor, an unfortunate event that had left little Shu with a terrible fear of seafood. Having graduated with a master's degree in French Literature from Peking University, Shu had managed to evade the Canadian authorities by relying on the same contortionist talents that had propelled her to the top of her class at the Shanghai Circus School, which she had chosen to attend after developing a disgust for all things literary. When the customs officers opened the shipping container where she was stowed away, she curled up into a ball then rolled silently into the port of Vancouver. A slimy sea snail had slipped into her onboard hideaway, forcing her to crouch alongside it for days on end, petrified and chilled to the bone, haunted by the memory of Grandma Li. She had chosen to go by the name of Misty rather than Shu ever since her debut night at the Nile, when Jasmine had introduced her—"And now from the Middle Kingdom, the ravishing, mysterious Shu!"—and one particular idiot had shouted out from the audience, "You know what they say, eh? If the Shu fits..." The crowd had laughed raucously at the distasteful remark, heaping shame upon the proud Chinese artist. Ever since that incident, she'd adopted the stage name Misty, the first word she'd learned in Vancouver, when a fan of old-school jazz, and of all things exotic and delightful in general, had welcomed her into his home. Met with silence by the stranger who spoke only Mandarin and could barely say her own name in English, the good Samaritan had said, "I'll call you Misty, like the song. Do you know Ella Fitzgerald? You prefer Sarah Vaughan? You know the song... I get misty, whenever you're near..." He then proceeded to play her both versions in full, starting with Ella Fitzgerald. Shu-Misty didn't understand a word, but she liked it. She wondered how the same song could pass from the sun to the moon from one mouth to the next, how the same words, robbed of all meaning, could either light up or devour the soul. Something in the voices touched her in a place where she hadn't been touched often enough.

71

Realizing that the bachelor was beginning to have feelings for her that she would never be able to reciprocate, Shu-Misty slipped out a crack in the window one night. Of her first Canadian benefactor, she had kept nothing but her new name. Unlike the first two acts, hers was all grace and languidness, accompanied by the steady beat of Chinese drums. She was in the habit of bounding off the stage after a full striptease that revealed her perfect body, which she would twist, tie up in knots, and fold as she pleased, while the crowd oohed and aahed at her astonishing flexibility.

"Hot! Hot! Hot! Please welcome Suzie and Mimi!" To the pounding of tams-tams, the girls from Angola and Mozambique—the polar opposite of the pearl of the Far East—cranked up the heat on the testosterone soup that the audience had been reduced to and brought it to the boil. Perhaps it was the ostrich feathers that struggled to contain their magnificent breasts or maybe it was the way Suzie slapped Mimi's bottom. Either way, the Conservative MPs for Nova Scotia were driven to distraction, dousing themselves in beer to quench the flames of lust that threatened to consume them. "Oh, dear God!" the well-mannered Maritimers chorused.

Moved to paroxysms of pleasure, the spectators began smashing chairs over each other's heads to let off a little steam, at which point Carlota and Roberta from Santiago de Cuba made their appearance, shuddering and shaking to the music of an ear-splitting salsa, caressing every inch of each other's coffee-coloured skin. When their number was over, Carlota produced a Havana cigar from her jet-black hair, biting off the tip and spitting it into the audience before, hands on hips, allowing her partner to introduce it into an orifice that God had certainly not intended for that purpose, lighting it with a lighter held aloft by a volunteer who tried, in vain, not to lose his mind, trembling and sighing heavily as he returned to his seat with the cigar, which he savoured pensively for the rest of the evening while the Université de Montréal profs cried, "Revolución!"

"And now, the lady behind this unforgettable spectacle. Gentlemen, please welcome, Djaaazmiiiine!"

To end the show, Jasmine, the stunning performer with chestnut-brown eyes whose looks had practically convinced the entire McGill University law faculty to sign up as one to the Marxist-Leninist Party of Quebec, came on stage dressed as a *fille du roi* to the sounds of *O Canada* playing in the background. She commanded true patriot love in no time at all, while the audience stood on guard, right hands pressed to their hearts as they sang along. When she removed the final maple leaf covering her home and native land, the first bars of the *Internationale* rang out, and all the other strippers gathered around Jasmine to sing, in Russian, French, then English, the glorious hymn of revolutionaries the world over. The show closed to the strains of "The international ideal unites the human race," as the crowd roared its approval. It was always at that very moment that several of the men would have to be carried out on stretchers, men who, barely an hour earlier, appeared well on track to live another half-century. Before the next performance started, Jasmine thanked, in both official languages, Canada's Minister of Multiculturalism for approving the artists' visas and for the funding that made the show possible. The applause went on, louder than ever, until the curtain came down over the ten beauties. When it finally petered out, a young, clear voice rang out from the bar: "Bravo! Bravo! Enggore! Enggore! What a performance!"

Perched on the shoulders of Joey Laframboise, a mustachioed foreman employed by the Lantic Sugar Company, sat little Rosa in her mauve dress. She was clapping for all she was worth, tears welling in her eyes. She'd been enraptured by what she'd seen, by the sight of so many people standing side by side, adulating the symbols of her childhood and adolescence. She had been absorbed in every second of it. At that moment she wished that time would stand still, that this feeling would last forever. She'd never had such fun. Never again would she spend her Thursday nights playing Scrabble. She could no longer contain her tears of joy. Joey grinned in amusement and bought her a crème de menthe to help calm her nerves. "It's like this every night at the Nile," he told her. All eyes were now trained on Rosa. Everyone assumed that she was a surprise addition to the show and would be performing from the bar during the intermission. Quite oblivious to the fact that she was being undressed a million times over by lecherous eyes, Rosa flashed her perfect smile. "Workers of the world, unite!" she yelled, raising her glass. She hadn't even brought the drink to her lips when Jeanne Joyal grabbed her by the ear and dragged her out of the den of iniquity.

"Have you lost your mother-loving mind?" she exploded, but Rosa was still awash in the blissful waters of the Nile.

"Jeanne! What are you doing here? Where are we going? There's gonna be another show soon."

"Would you mind explaining how you managed to wind up in the biggest dive in Montreal in less than twenty-four hours? I was worried. The Indian guy at the front desk sent me here. Said he thought he'd seen you with those girls. Tell me he was wrong, for the love of God. Get in the van, I'm takin' you home. That's enough of that."

"But why are we leaving? Didn't you ligge the show?"

"*Like!* The word is *like!* And there's nothing to like about it. What goes on at the Nile is degrading to women everywhere! The cops've been trying to shut the joint down for years. A good thing I went in there to drag you away from its hellish clutches. You wouldn't be the first girl to leave her soul behind!"

"Maybe it was the musigg you were less ggeen on. Jasmine ggould worgg a little harder on the transitions, I have to admit. And, if you asgg me, I'm not sure Tatiana and Ludmilla should open the show. If we're going to stay true to the timeline, Blondie and Nelly should really have gone first. Marx was German, after all. What do you thingg, Jeanne?"

"I think you've lost your mind. You came here to get the wind to pick up, not to be hanging around in seedy downtown hotels with a bunch of wayward women. Now, my girl, it's time for bed. We can talk about it tomorrow morning. I don't wanna hear another damn word outta that mouth of yours."

Speeding north through the dark of night, Jeanne Joyal didn't take her eyes off Boulevard Saint-Laurent for a second, so caught up in the moment that she even ran a red light or two. She turned right, then left into an alleyway, and led Rosa into a red-brick house that melted into all the other homes on Saint-Ciboire in the darkness. Fast asleep beneath the street lights, the street looked for all the world like two rows of trees, their leaves turned orange by fall, lined by two identical walls that were interrupted only by wooden doors at regular intervals. Rosa tiptoed in after her landlady.

"Try not to wake up the other lodgers. A young girl arrived earlier this evening while I was waiting for you. You'll share your room with her. She doesn't look like she'll disturb you. My room's on the ground floor."

Upstairs, Rosa could make out four doors off a hallway, plus an impeccably folded pile of towels sitting on a table.

"Bathroom's to your right. That's Jacqueline's room next to it. Heather's room is to the left. You've got the room with the new girl who's already asleep by now. Don't wake her up. She looked like she'd been having a rough time of things when she begged me to rent her the room."

The room contained two single beds, and Rosa could just make out the outline of a figure beneath the covers that rose and fell with her gentle breathing. Jeanne pressed a finger to her lips, then slowly closed the door.

Rosa was so exhausted she didn't even undress before falling into a deep, deep sleep.

::

In Notre-Dame-du-Cachalot, something incredible had happened to upset the deathly quiet in the village: a letter arrived from Montreal, addressed to Aunt Zenaida. It was Napoleon, the postmaster and guardian of the covered bridge, who first saw it. There hadn't been anything like it in over twelve years, not since the day Mayor Duressac was sent a secret communiqué from GLUM. Napoleon hadn't had a single letter to deliver in the village since 1988. And so, unless the envelope was stamped SECRET, Napoleon made a song and dance about every delivery. Clutching the letter in both hands, his eyes wide as sea urchins, he ran off to seek the advice of Mayor Duressac, who asked his secretary what she thought, who mentioned it to her sister-in-law Juliette. By the end of the afternoon, every man, woman, and child in the village had learned that the Canadian postal service, which had never deigned to give the godforsaken village so much as a postal code, had just recognized its existence by delivering a letter there. The mayor was somewhat disconcerted by the turn of events but, good socialist that he was, he knew that he could leave it up to the bureaucrats to guide him. He eventually dredged up a dusty old municipal by-law that set out exactly what was to be done were such a thing ever to happen. Unless the letter had the word SECRET stamped directly below the postmark, it was to be opened and read out loud before the whole village. And so it was with a twinge of regret that Duressac set down the particularly flattering biography of Yves Montand he was in the midst of to organize a public reading of the letter. Napoleon was tasked with rounding up the villagers.

"It's a letter for old Zenaida!"

"Saints preserve us! It ggan only be from our little Rosa. Napoleon, go asgg Miss Nordet to ring the sggool bell. Little Rosa must have very important news for us!"

The villagers emerged from their hiding places, risking life and limb to gather in the parish hall. Old Zenaida was dragged away from her knitting. The letter was to be read before the entire village, and the person to whom it was addressed had to be present. Someone draped a shawl over her to shield her from the fumes of Boredom and sat her down on the stage in a rocking chair, where she could get on with her knitting. Mayor Duressac called for silence, explained to his constituents that a letter from Montreal, no doubt penned by Rosa's hand, had just arrived at the village post office and most likely contained encouraging news from the brave girl. He sliced open the envelope with a shellfish, unfolded the sheets of blue paper that were covered in feverish writing, and began to read the missive, the audience hanging on his every word. For the simple reason that Rosa wrote every *d* and *u* just the way Terese had, it took everything Duressac had not to shed a tear of nostalgia.

Montreal, September 27, 2000
Dear Aunt Zenaida,
I'm so exhausted that my hand is shagging as I write
these lines. I should be asleep and I badly need the rest,
but instead I am tagging advantage of a lull at worgg
to send you my news.

"My God, she's at worgg!" Napoleon interrupted.
"She's found a job! She really is just ligge her mother,
ggan't sit still for a minute!"

Napoleon was politely invited to keep his opinions
to himself. The mayor cleared his throat and continued
reading the letter in a tone of voice worthy of a notary
public:

First, I really must say, dear aunt, how much I regret
the way we left each other. I heard your voice eggoing
in my head long after we parted, far beyond the bridge
over the Massaggre River. It breaggs my heart to know
that you are all alone in the village, where death lurggs
at every turn, demanding saggrifices be made day in,
day out. I hope that the good mayor Duressagg is ggeep-
ing an eye on you, just as he promised me he would
before I left. Since Mom died, he's really the only one
left in the village that we ggan ggount on.

There were rumblings of discontent. The people of
Notre-Dame-du-Cachalot tutted and looked around at
each other. Embarrassed, the mayor continued:

79

However ggan I eggxplain all that has happened to me ever since Napoleon toogg my photo? Let's just say that Mom would no doubt have said it was a Great Leap Forward! But I still haven't figured out a way to raise the west wind.

"So what's she doing? Organizing a union?" an anonymous, embittered, and sarcastic male voice inquired.

I've been inggredibly luggy to meet Jeanne Joyal, an eggceptional woman who welggomes hard-worgging young girls into her home in return for a modest rent. Montreal is eggxperiencing a housing ggrisis at the moment, and I ggonsider myself very fortunate not to be living in a tent under Highway 40, ligge other people my age are doing. I've been living at Jeanne's for almost a month now. You'd ligge her. She embodies all the qualities that allow me to believe that one day things will change in this world of ours and the ggapitalist struggtures will ggrumble beneath the force of our labour. If Jeanne's ggourage and ggharaggter were ggontagious diseases, let's just say that the socialist paradise we enjoy in Notre-Dame-du-Ggachalot would have spread all over the world by now. You will understand, dear aunt, when I ggonfess that I agreed to let Jeanne lend me some money so that I ggan dress ligge a Montrealer. People were really starting to give my 1912 pantsuit strange looggs.

An exasperated "Pfff" went up in the audience.

Speagging of ggourage, dear aunt, I found myself a job in Montreal the very night I arrived! I'm a night receptionist and ggontroller at the Butler Motor Hotel (Jeanne's always saying the name of the hotel should be in French: l'Hôtel du majordome motorisé!), a small downtown hotel where Jasmine stays—she's a very well-known performer who's beggome my friend. I run the front desgg and magge sure that the booggs balance at the end of every night. The manager, a charming man from India, toogg me at my word when I told him I'd done the same job in Percé. He hired me on the spot.

One of the villagers, who was suffering from a particularly stubborn case of cynicism, interrupted the mayor with a spiteful remark. "So now she's lying to land herself a job! I wonder what her mother would have said about *that!*" Everyone pretended not to have heard.

I must admit I'm sorry I lied... Aggounting is more ggompliggated than I ever thought. But I have to earn a living, as Jeanne ggeeps telling me. That's one of the many reasons I admire her: she doesn't beat about the bush. She's not one to be handing out charity to poor homeless girls—that wouldn't get them far!

"Give a man a fish and he'll eat for a day. Teach a man to fish and you feed him for a lifetime," Zenaida interrupted sagely, glancing up from the purple sweater she was knitting. The audience grunted in agreement.

81

She doesn't go in for ggondescending charity, as so many others in the city do, alienating individuals from their material lives. Jeanne worggs hard for what she has, and she eggspeggts no less from her boarders. You should see her! She's all worgg, worgg, worgg. Her day starts at five in the morning, when the whole house is still fast asleep (apart from me). And she doesn't stop until eleven o'gglogg at night. Jeanne Joyal is living proof that humanggind was made to worgg, that we are fulfilled through and by our worgg. That attachment to worgg, which was so ggruelly lagging in our village and led to the paper mill gglosing, Jeanne ggould bring it bagg.

The audience let out a flurry of indignant "ohs," "huhs," and "well I nevers."

Tagge this morning. It was Heather's turn to do the dishes after breggfast. Well, the lazy thing only washed them, leaving them to dry on the ragg! Jeanne always tagges the time to ggarefully wipe everything dry with a gglean towel then put it away. Jeanne didn't mince her words. "If you're gonna half-ass it, don't do it at all," she told her. And she's quite right, when you thingg about it. Did Heather thingg the dishes were going to dry themselves then float through the air and into the ggupboards? Jeanne summoned all the boarders to the ggitchen to repeat how the dishes were to be washed. "Here in Gguebegg, we dry the dishes. We don't leave them to dry on the ggounter, ligge they do in Ontario!

We're gglean folgg!" she eggsplained. She reminded me so much of Mom!

Along with Heather—a student from Windsor, Ontario, with sea-blue eyes—there's Jaggueline, a friendly Haitian girl from Port-au-Prince, who spends her days teaching philosophy at a high sggool. And there's Perdita, a girl from Guruistan, who's studying math at the University of Montreal. I share my room with her. And let me tell you, Heather's in the right place to learn French. Jeanne ggaught her chatting in English the other day with Jaggueline, who speaggs French, English, Spanish, and Portuguese. Jeanne was quigg to remind her of the house rules. "Speagg French with her! You're in Montreal, not Toronto!" And the two of them switched to French. I'm sure it's down to women ligge Jeanne that we still speagg French in this ggountry. Sometimes when Jeanne's in the ggitchen and we're all sitting in silence around the table, waiting for our soup, she'll shout out to us to speagg French. We don't dare ggontradiggt her. We don't want to magge her feel unggomfortable. I thingg it must be the ggids playing in the alleyway behind the house that she hears. A few of them must speagg English.

"And the wind? What about the wind? When's the wind gonna put in an appearance? When we're all dead and gone?"

Miss Nordet had jumped to her feet to fire off the question. Émilie Nordet always spoke in a cutting tone that made the blood run cold, like the rest of the Nordet family, who had been teachers for seven generations.

Duressac glowered at the schoolmistress, who realized that she had just lost a little of the respect that the population had always paid her as a teacher.

My dear auntie, rest assured: my search goes on. I know that patience is a virtue, but sometimes I'd just ligge everything to be sorted out so that I ggan go bagg home and live a normal life. I don't know how many times I'm going to hear the same reply: "I don't know where this wind is that you're talgging about, miss. I've never heard tell of such a thing. Perhaps you should ggall Environment Gganada?" But the good people of our village will soon have to hold on to their hats with both hands, just ligge they did bagg in the day, believe you me. I ggan see a ggouple ggoming over to the front desgg. I'll leave you for now, dear aunt. I promise you, I ggan do this. I don't know how just yet, but I know I'll get there in the end."
Your little Rosa
xxx

The old lady set down her knitting needles and wiped away a tear. She was handed the letter then escorted back home. The villagers were left deflated by the rather glum news from Montreal and scuttled back to their little wooden homes. Left alone in the parish hall, Duressac and Napoleon exchanged meaningful looks. The mayor sighed, holding his head in both hands.

"Poor Rosa! Poor, poor little Rosa! Maybe I should've gone myself."

"Listen, Mr. Mayor. Just give her time—she'll figure it out. She's got more brains than the rest of us put together."

"But will it be enough, Napoleon? Will it be enough?"

The two men went home and were surprised to find themselves asking out loud, at precisely the same time, what the blazes a butler motor might be.

::

Meanwhile, back at the hotel, Rosa was having a difficult time of things. Every evening, when she got to work, the hotel register would already be full of the plainest names imaginable. Tonight she'd spotted yet another Mr. and Mrs. Smith from Ottawa, a Monsieur and Madame Tremblay from Trois-Rivières, and even a Hernández or two go by. The hotel must have come highly recommended in all the beauty product magazines because all the wives who stayed there inevitably wore their makeup like a Japanese Noh mask. The husbands tended to wander back outside alone, no doubt in search of a bite to eat. Then the women would also leave by themselves, returning to the hotel in the company of other men who wouldn't look Rosa in the eye, and this merry dance would go on until four o'clock in the morning. The weekends were the busiest. But Rosa didn't concern herself with getting to the bottom of the strange procession. She was too busy balancing the hotel's books, a simple piece of accounting that nevertheless took her hours, so befuddled was she by the dance of numbers and lines. Rosa hadn't spent the past month sitting on her hands, mind you. As well as teaching herself the basics of accounting, she had managed to rid herself almost entirely of her Gaspé accent, by doing a series of daily exercises. Now it only came racing back when her emotions were running high, at moments of great hesitation or the utmost weariness. She had no intention of being made fun of ever again in a store, the clerk inquiring if she'd like some salted cod when she'd asked for "gguggumbers." The jibe had been hard to swallow, sticking painfully in her throat like the disagreeable feeling that lingers after a violent bout of vomiting. She was standing alone behind her counter, nibbling on a pen and leaning on an elbow, wondering which column the gas bill should go in, when a youthful-sounding voice made her jump with fright.

"You have a problem?"

It was one of the three Mrs. Smiths who'd just come back, this one by far the youngest and most attractive of the bunch. A short redhead who always wore the same orange leather miniskirt and black lace bra.

"Uh... no, no," Rosa lied.

The fact of the matter was, she was wondering whether the heating oil should be filed under accounts payable or in one of the dozens of other columns in the huge ledger.

Mrs. Smith spoke like Heather did, with an accent that always made it seem to Rosa as though they were swallowing every *l*.

"What's yer name?"

"Rosa."

"That's nice. I'm Gillian. From New York City. I used to work in Paris, but I had to get outta there. The Eastern European girls were driving prices down like you wouldn't believe. I just couldn't make a decent living, you know. Where are you from? You're new around here. I never saw you before last week."

Although normally in such a rush, running around all night doing errands that could never seem to wait until morning, Gillian took the time to listen to Rosa's story from beginning to end. She was fascinated. Rosa was pleased to have made a new friend and invited Gillian to sit with her in the back office, where she could still keep an eye on the front desk through the one-way mirror.

"So, where's your husband, Gillian Smith?" she asked in all seriousness. "I just saw him leave."

Gillian gave her the look of an unbeliever who's just seen Christ emerge from the tomb.

"What husband? I'm not married!"

"But what about Mr. Smith?"

"Hahh! Those are just names we use: Smith, Thompson, Tremblay... Do you think the johns are honestly going to check in under their real names?"

"Oh. So, where's John Smith?"

"What cave have you been living in, girl? Do you really have no idea what goes on in this shithole?"

Rosa was stunned. Had things been going on during her shift? She had to know!

"Um. Well, uh, I *had* noticed that the guests weren't getting much sleep."

"Thank God! Can you imagine if they fell asleep afterwards on top of everything else? As if we had the time! You pay *by the hour* at this hotel, Rosa. Do you even know what that means?"

"Well, I suppose it helps people save money."

Gillian had the distinct impression she was dealing with a complete halfwit.

"Me and the other girls, we bring the johns back here to the Butler. The manager lets us get on with it since he knows this dive is only a tax dodge for the owner anyway. Word is, he's an influential minister in Ottawa."

"A minister! Maybe he can help me find the wind."

"I don't think that's his style. He's a bit of an S.O.B., by the sound of things. You won't find the wind here at the Butler, take my word for it."

"I wasn't planning to. But tell me one thing, would you? How do you keep all those Johns straight? Doesn't it get confusing? A John Smith here, a John Smith there?"

Gillian burst out laughing. A genuine laugh from a pretty woman is worth ten normal laughs, and it's all the more contagious for it. Rosa shared a good laugh with her new friend from New York. Their laughter faded slowly, picked up a little, then died a natural death. Gillian took both of Rosa's wrists in her hands and looked her straight in the eye, the same way a mother might sit a young child down to explain once and for all that Grandad won't be coming back and that he's off for a nice long sleep.

"Listen up, Rosa darling. You're the funniest girl I've met in this city. I like you. You're sweet. Okay, so there are no John Smiths in this hotel, only johns. Me and the other girls, we work the corner at Sainte-Catherine and Saint-Laurent. We bring our customers back to the Butler so we don't have to do it in a back alley somewhere. Those places are crawling with cops. We're hookers. Working girls. Sex workers. Capeesh?"

Albert Einstein's eyes surely couldn't have grown any wider than Rosa's when he first realized that E = MC². She began to giggle. And the laughter picked up again. A fierce womanly laughter. It lasted as long as it might take you to work your way through the editorial page of a very serious newspaper and then polish off the crossword to boot. It left them exhausted and satisfied, like sated lovers.

"You mean it only takes you ten minutes?"

"Well, we're not going to spend all night sending John Smith on his way. We have overheads, you know."

"Ten minutes to get into bed, to do... it, get dressed, and come back downstairs?"

"What do you mean, get into bed? My God, we don't go near the bed! We don't so much as get undressed. That way, if the cops show up, we can always say we're just friends."

"Ah, I see. But what do you do?"

"We work on our knees. It's our specialty. We're the best in town."

"And you can earn a living like that?"

"Let's just say, on a good night, when there's a Conservative party convention in town, say, you can make around two thousand bucks."

"I don't even make that in a month!"

"Yeah, but look at the shitty job you're stuck with. What are all those numbers about? I hate math. I studied literature in New York before doing this. I'm made for the night life. Look, can I trust you? You won't go running to the cops?"

"No! No! Never. A woman has a right to do whatever she wants with her body. That's what Mother used to say."

"Listen, Rosa, I'll send Cassandra over to help with your math problem. She studied accounting before packing it in to join my team. I've gotta go now. Duty calls. Those jobs aren't gonna blow themselves. *Ciao bella,* as they say around here!"

A brothel. Rosa was working in a brothel. She'd left behind the Scrabble games and gentle mists of her village to wind up as a receptionist in a brothel. So, apart from Jasmine and her band of showgirls, there was only one other kind of guest staying at the hotel. Something told her that what Gillian had just told her was not to be shared with another soul. Least of all Jeanne Joyal, who spent part of each day lecturing the boarders about the importance of respecting their bodies and the abuses women around the world were subjected to.

Gillian kept her promise. Cassandra, the bookkeeping lady of the night, showed up at the front desk fifteen minutes after Gillian left.

"So, I hear there are books to be balanced?"

It took Cassandra twenty minutes to sort out what Rosa had been grappling with for six long nights. Rosa looked on in admiration as the streetwalker with the washed-out blue hair, all while chain-smoking and chewing her gum in a more provocative fashion than Rosa had ever seen, totted up, multiplied, and balanced the figures.

"There you go. All done, darling."

"So that's what it was! I kept forgetting about the petty cash and it just wouldn't add up. Where did you learn to do that?"

"HEC Montreal."

"And you have to walk the streets to survive?"

"Survive? Who said anything about surviving? I've worked for some of the biggest companies in Toronto. I saw more money pass through my hands than you can imagine. I earned in one month three times what the prime minister makes in a year."

"Why did you leave then?"

"Do you know what it's like working with those men all day? When it came down to it, all I was doing was helping them pass off as securities the heaps of money they were making organ trafficking in the third world. I couldn't look myself in the mirror anymore. Then, one day I decided to blow the whistle..."

"And?"

"They found out. I had to run. I took off, changed my name. Gillian found me here one night and ever since I've been Cassandra, the blue-haired hooker on Sainte-Catherine Street."

"That's so tragic!"

"Tragic? Let me tell you something, sweetie: I'd rather be screwing men than trafficking their body parts. And let me tell you another thing. You seem like a smart girl. Money is a cancer. It doesn't matter if the big guns are giving it to you to cover their asses at some accounting firm in Toronto, or paying you with it in some seedy hotel in Montreal, it's all the same money."

"Money has no smell! That's what my old aunt used to say."

"To be honest, all those bills I stuff down my bra every night end up smelling like they've come in off the street, but at least they're not covered in blood and tears."

Cassandra looked sad. Rosa thanked her for her help for the hundredth time.

"Easy as pie, hon. Any time."

Gillian and Cassandra had a busy night. As she watched them come back in every ten minutes with the ever uglier, ever shabbier dregs from the bottom of the barrel, Rosa exchanged knowing looks with her new friends. Behind the desk, she pinched her right butt cheek hard to stop herself laughing. Night after night, Rosa looked on as Cassandra and Gillian waltzed by with their "fifteen-minute husbands," an experience that gave her a close-up view of the nature of mankind, despite knowing nothing herself of skinship, only what the ill-informed gossip of the girls at school had taught her. Terese had never taken the time to sit down with her and explain how she had come into the world. Rosa had pictured a thousand different scenarios gleaned from the schmaltzy romance novels in the school library and from a book that Miss Nordet loaned out to every girl on her thirteenth birthday: *I Am a Woman*. Normally kept under lock and key in the old spinster's desk, the book would be loaned for seven days. Miss Nordet and her bun didn't mess around when it came to books. She'd once been spotted descending on the Crachin home in search of a comic book that young Kevin hadn't returned on time. And so, on May 20, 1993, Rosa had received the book, carefully covered in brown paper, from the hands of her teacher. Engrossed in her pile of newspapers all week long, Rosa had forgotten all about the book and, torn between drawing Miss Nordet's ire and spending the rest of her days in complete and utter ignorance, she had returned the book without so much as opening it. There are some books you regret not having read for the rest of your life. *I Am a Woman* topped the list of books Rosa wished she'd read, right up there with Émile Zola's *Thérèse Raquin* and Lenin's *Against Right-wing and Left-wing Opportunism, Against Trotskyism*. Rosa had always suspected that one day her negligence would come back to haunt her, and that night had shown her as much. Miss Nordet's book had no doubt spared no detail when it came to blue-haired hookers and their johns.

CHAPTER 3

Revolution for Dummies

WHEN SHE WASN'T WORKING AT THE HOTEL and her land-lady allowed her an evening off, Rosa would travel the length and breadth of Montreal in search of the wind. She began by climbing to the top of Mount Royal, where she realized that the air over the city was as static as it had been in her village. Not so much as a puff. Nobody seemed the least bit concerned, though. The talk of the town was the death of Pierre Elliott Trudeau, a for-mer prime minister whom Rosa had heard very little of outside of Miss Nordet's history lessons. She vaguely remembered asking her mother about the man whose name appeared below a photo in her history textbook. Terese, normally so eager to respond to any general knowledge question, had raised her hackles at the mere mention of the former prime minister's name. "Finish your homework," she'd ordered. Rosa had taken that to mean that certain words were forbidden in Terese's home. Which is why she never asked about who her father was, or who was prime minister of Canada on the day she was born. Zenaida, who had witnessed the scene, muttered to Rosa: "Let sleeping dogs lie."

On that October 3, 2000, after a night's work, and with deep circles beneath her eyes, Rosa had followed the crowd to Place d'Armes. Notre-Dame Basilica was filled to the brim with heads of state, while the commoners followed the funeral outside on a giant screen. She wandered around like a zombie among the crowds come to pay their respects to the deceased. It would have been easy to mistake her for a mourner. In front of the basilica, limousines spat out presidents and princes. And that was the day she caught sight of what she at first took to be a mirage. She rubbed her eyes as she drew closer, but they weren't deceiving her. It was Fidel Castro standing a hundred metres from her. She let out a little shriek, raised a fist, and went to cry out. But the revolutionary was already disappearing into the basilica. Rosa waited and waited. People who had travelled from far and wide stared at her as she stood there stiff as a statue, tears streaming down her face. A journalist from Victoria honed in on the tears, snapping her photo as she stood there in complete stupefaction, and the following day Rosa's grieving face appeared on the front page of a British Columbia newspaper, along with the caption: "Montrealers Mourn Trudeau." Nobody on the other side of the beautiful Rocky Mountains that Rosa hadn't lost in the 1980 independence referendum would ever know that the tears had nothing to do with the late prime minister, and everything to do with Rosa's joy at seeing, for the first and likely only time, a true revolutionary on French-Canadian soil. For the longest time, Rosa waited in vain for the Cuban to re-emerge from the church. When she asked people in the crowd if they knew how to get the wind to pick up, they assumed she had gone mad with grief. They were partly right. Revolutionaries and photographs are so often misunderstood.

The days passed. As she walked along Boulevard Saint-Laurent or pressed her forehead against the cold window of the number 55 bus, Rosa would devote a good chunk of her mental energy to getting her bearings. Over the past few weeks, her personal story had taken off at lightning speed. The fact that everything had happened in September and October wasn't lost on her. But she resisted the temptation to call it a revolution. She wasn't for turning: a revolution was an abrupt and violent toppling of a regime, leading to profound transformations in the political organization of a society. Period. That's it, that's all. Gillian had taught her the expression *that's it, that's all*. She liked it, since it allowed her to put an end to all kinds of indecision. She had spoken to Jasmine about it, and Jasmine had encouraged her to be more flexible in her definition of revolution. "After all, you could say that fall 2000 marked Rosa Ost's very own personal revolution." Although Rosa was flattered at the thought, more than anything she feared losing a handle on a sacred term that she wasn't prepared to apply to mundane concerns. At least a few people would have to die before there could be talk of revolution. And, aside from Terese and the others who had succumbed to Boredom back in Notre-Dame-du-Cachalot, people weren't exactly dropping like flies.

Our little Rosa wasn't used to leading a complicated existence. She recalled that, scarcely a few months previously, her life had been one of disarming simplicity and reassuring routine: reading Marx, playing Scrabble, learning new proverbs, and walking along the shore as she looked out at the horizon. Ever since Jeanne Joyal had added her to her crazy gang on Route 132, everything had become so much more complicated. Not a day would go by without some new and eccentric character bursting into her life, revealing another facet of humanity that her native village had kept hidden from her. Rosa resorted to making bookmarks that she would stuff in her copy of *Capital*, consulting them regularly to help her keep track of the Fellini-esque tangle of players. The first bookmark, the one she'd decorated with a red star, listed each and every one of Lenin's Great-Granddaughters, plus their country of origin, since she tended to mix them up. Sometimes she'd be deep in discussion with one of the strippers and would have to glance down at her book, just to be sure she had her name right. To the list she'd added the names of Gillian and Cassandra, the two friendly streetwalkers who kept her entertained between turning tricks on long nights at the Butler Motor Hotel. And so it was that the bookmark bore the names of every woman who resided at the hotel. Rosa couldn't help but feel a certain sense of pride every time she looked at the list. As the hotel's night receptionist, she knew everything that went on there. She followed all the comings and goings and, had she been more of an entrepreneur, could easily have lined her pockets by blackmailing the johns. Instead, Rosa contented herself with fleecing the hotel owner by way of a pact she had with Gillian and Cassandra. Since the girls did no more than get down on their knees on the carpet, it was easy to say they'd never set foot in the rooms. So, she made a deal with them: The first john would pay for the room, Rosa would pretend to note it in the ledger, then she'd erase it the following morning once she'd checked that the room was still as good as new. That way Rosa would pocket at least seventy dollars every night. Her salary added up to only a thousand dollars a month, and Jeanne got five hundred of that. Her new wardrobe had cost her three hundred. The rest she sent to Zenaida, who was stuck back in Notre-Dame-du-Cachalot with no means of support. So things were a bit tight. She also had to pay for a transit pass and the odd secondhand book from the store on Avenue Mont-Royal. Bending the rules like that allowed her to double her salary and to live an almost normal life in a city that had no use for people like her. Needless to say, there was no prospect of a promotion or a better career move.

The second, smaller bookmark bore the names of the lodgers who stayed with Jeanne. Given that they were fewer in number, it was easier for Rosa to remember their names. Jeanne wasn't easily forgettable. Jacqueline was the first Black person Rosa had ever met. Heather, the bilingual Canadian with the deadpan sense of humour, had opened the door to the boundless west for Rosa, who had never travelled. As for Perdita, she had managed to shroud in mystery an already disarming sense of otherness. Originally from Guruistan, a former Soviet republic in the war-torn Caucasus, the young woman always draped herself in navy blue shawls until only her eyes could be seen. In addition to the dull math textbooks she loved, Perdita enjoyed reading the verses of the late Shah Gidogstori, her country's spiritual leader. From time to time, she would chant a few sacred verses, of which Rosa didn't understand a word. The verses, apparently, were incredibly precise prophecies that spelled out the story of humanity from beginning to end. The prophet had so far predicted the industrial revolution, the sinking of the *Titanic*, the moon landing, the passing of a number of comets, and all the major wars.

The nights of October and the first half of November passed in this fashion. Rosa kept on asking if anyone happened to know, by any chance, how to raise the west wind. All she got in return were blank looks, head shakes, and pointed fingers. Her life consisted of working from midnight to eight o'clock the next morning at the Butler, taking the number 55 bus from the corner of Sainte-Catherine and Saint-Laurent, getting off at Jarry, and making for her bed on Saint-Ciboire, exhausted from her night of number-crunching, hustlers, and coffee. She would only just have time to say hello to Perdita as she left for school. Rosa would fall asleep gazing at the winkle on her chest of drawers, not that it had said a word since leaving the beach at Notre-Dame-du-Cachalot. "Well, say something," she'd sigh before she dozed off. More often than not, she'd sleep right through the day, getting up at six in the evening when Perdita breezed into her room. "Time to get up, Rosa! You'll be late for supper!" Jeanne did not tolerate tardiness. "I'm regular as clockwork, so I am!" she'd told Jacqueline pointedly one Wednesday night when she'd turned up five minutes late for her landlady's signature braised beef, a meal that had been masticated in dismayed silence.

Anyone who'd failed to notice that life at Jeanne Joyal's was regular as clockwork would have been very distracted indeed. Each and every meal was served at precisely the same hour, according to a five-day rotating schedule that the landlady proudly declared hadn't changed in decades. This allowed her, she said, to work out her operating costs weeks in advance and to not waste time wondering what she was going to cook. True to form, Jeanne's cuisine was family style: honest and forthright. Rosa knew by heart the menu that Jeanne had pinned to the dining-room wall. Written in ink on time-worn paper, the menu was followed like a commandment from on high. "Planned home economics. Now that's an interesting start," Rosa had said to herself the first time she read it. After a month in Montreal, she no longer needed a watch or a calendar. "Thursday: Irish stew," she would hear Heather sigh in despair.

That Monday, there was a lovely surprise waiting on the table for Rosa: someone had mailed her a parcel.

She recognized Aunt Zenaida's ancient scrawl in a flash. The good woman had knitted her a lilac sweater that Jacqueline immediately envied. At the bottom of the box, which still bore a fresh and clean grandmotherly smell, Rosa discovered a postcard from Notre-Dame-du-Cachalot. There was only one postcard of the place in existence: a panorama of the sun setting over the village. To the far left of the dune, Rosa could make out her house, the school, the church, and all the rest of the village; and to the right, the Three Sisters, the closed paper mill, and the covered bridge. She turned the postcard over and gazed at the stamp with La Bolduc on it.

Rosa burst out crying.

La Bolduc was smiling up at God.

Mondays always ended with an introduction to Quebec history. Not content with simply providing affordable room and board for young women, Jeanne was determined to educate and entertain them, too. Which meant that each night of the week was organized around a cultural theme. Well aware that many of her boarders weren't from the province, Jeanne used these evenings to help ease their passage into Quebec society. She would tell jokes over supper that Rosa found hilarious the first week, not understanding why her housemates weren't laughing along, too. By the second week, she'd realized that Jeanne's jokes followed a seven-day cycle. This meant that Jacqueline, for instance, who had been living at Jeanne's for three years, had heard more than one hundred and fifty-six times the one about the Newfie who didn't downhill ski because he couldn't find any sloped lakes where he lived. And it also meant that Heather, who had been living on Saint-Ciboire for five months, had been told twenty times, "Hey, Heather! I was waiting for my carrots to be delivered and do you know what happened?" God only knows why the Ontarian would invariably reply, an Oscar-worthy inquiring expression on her face: "Uh, I don't know, Jeanne. What happened?" To which Jeanne would wait for a beat, then say, "They didn't *turnip!*" followed by a hearty belly laugh that the girls would never fail to imitate. Rosa played along, not wanting to appear ungrateful by accusing Jeanne of trotting out the same old stories. She was glad to see that her housemates were as respectful of their elders as she was. Jeanne would then clear the table and disappear into the kitchen. Perdita, hidden but for her eyes, would clutch her head in both hands, while Heather and Jacqueline sighed dolefully.

Dessert was served every evening in Jeanne Joyal's parlour. The room, which took up the entire right side of the ground floor, was decorated simply. A huge armoire stood against the back wall, housing a television set, stereo, and a handful of books. This treasure was only ever unlocked at 7:30 p.m. on theme nights. The five women would sit in a circle. Jacqueline would struggle to keep her eyes open, Heather would allow her mind to wander off on an astral journey over the shores of Lake Erie to her native Essex County, while Perdita would work out in her head a particularly thorny algebraic equation. Only our little Rosa would listen attentively to Jeanne's presentation.

Jeanne had chosen to talk that evening about the Quiet Revolution, promising a musical interlude to wrap things up. The previous week, the housemates had been treated to a lecture entitled "*Je me souviens.* Chronicle of a cultural genocide," which described the ill treatment meted out to French-speaking Manitobans in the 1930s. This week, armed with an exhaustive three-volume history of Quebec published by an eminent historian at the University of Montreal, the landlady sought to educate her boarders about a turning point in the province's history. The lesson got underway with a detailed account of the trials and tribulations of Quebecers in the Duplessis era. There was no mention of what had come before that. The world had apparently started with Duplessis. The usual list of suspects followed: a stifling clergy, the perfidious English-speaking bourgeoisie, and a profit-obsessed corporate world. Then, as is always the case with such narratives, the election of Jean Lesage was identified as the catalyst for everything that followed. Year Zero. Jeanne reeled off Quebec's advances in education, public behaviour, and the nationalization of electricity. The 1960s had left their mark on Quebec more than anywhere else in the world, and Quebecers owed everything to that short spell when anything was possible, a time that had given birth to the Quebec we know today. Rosa was jubilant. Ever since leaving Notre-Dame-du-Cachalot behind, aside from Jasmine's wonderful show, her mind had found precious little to warrant serious reflection. Rosa had been used to long discussions with her mother on matters of much greater interest than the possibility of checking into a hotel under a different surname or mourning a former prime minister, and now Jeanne was offering an intellectual exchange that was a match for her curiosity. Unlike the other boarders, Rosa had no idea that Jeanne's talks were not intended as a springboard for discussion, but rather as exposés that left no room for questions. So, no one could begrudge Rosa for interrupting Jeanne's lecture with the following question:

"I've often wondered why it's called the 'Quiet Revolution.' Can it really be termed a revolution in the truest sense of the word? Was it not rather the manifestation, in French Canada, of a wave of profound change that all Western societies were experiencing? I mean, is it possible to speak of a 'revolution' as such? A revolution is either a revolution or it's not. Outside of poetry, a revolution cannot be quiet. And are we talking poetry or history? It's like referring to a scorching hot winter. It's a contradiction in terms..."

Jeanne stared at the young woman as though she'd lost her mind. Her fellow boarders wondered where she'd summoned up the courage. Jeanne tried to keep her emotions in check, tapping her foot against the wooden floor. Heather, clearly uneasy at the tension in the air, tried to come to Rosa's rescue.

"Uh... I think what Rosa means is that those societal changes, although sweeping and profound, were not exclusive to Quebec in the 1960s. For example, Ontario also went through a series of changes that was almost equally dramatic after the 1950s, although that period was never given any particular name. I think that Rosa is simply trying to situate the Quiet Revolution in a more global context, all while acknowledging the uniqueness of events in Quebec, because it's true that—"

Rosa, oblivious to the fact that Heather was throwing her a lifeline, cut her off, slipping deeper and deeper into the bog of her own presumptuousness.

"No, Heather, it's quite the opposite. First off, I do wish people would stop calling it a revolution. There've been revolutions in Cuba, France, and Russia, but not Quebec. What we had was a shift towards social democracy after a government was legitimately elected. Society's foundations didn't crumble. If we really wanted to call it a revolution, we'd have to call it the Failed Revolution, not the Quiet Revolution."

Heather, Perdita, and Jacqueline held their breaths. Rosa was beyond saving, not without incriminating themselves and risking being thrown out on their ear into the dark and damp Montreal night. Their landlady rose slowly from her chair. Then, like a spider circling around a fly it has just caught in its web, looked at each of the tenants one by one. Jacqueline wondered which of the four would be devoured first. Jeanne took a deep breath, arms folded, training her gaze first on Rosa, then Jacqueline, then Perdita and Heather. She stopped in front of the stereo. In a crude attempt at a national radio voice, she purred:

"Well then. Since our failed revolution appears to be of no interest whatsoever to our new arrival, perhaps we should try to find a little entertainment for that sophisticated mind of hers. Shall we listen to some music? How about the new Renard album?"

Jacqueline bit her clenched fist at the sound of the singer's name, her eyes rolling back in her head like she'd just been guillotined while Jeanne put on the CD. Rosa could sense she'd hit a nerve. But it wasn't her fault if everyone kept going around calling things revolutions. Who could blame her for wanting to preserve the meaning of a word that meant so much to her? And now Jeanne was refusing to talk about history and insisting on playing music instead. Well, music is good for the soul, Rosa thought to herself. No doubt this singer she'd never heard of would ease the tension and return Jeanne's parlour to its normally peaceful state.

"I'll play you a song that was number one in *France* for fourteen weeks. This is Renard, with *So Alone.*"

Rosa's top lip curled at the first words of the song that she had pinned her hopes on saving the evening. A rasping, inebriated, gravelly voice croaked out platitude after platitude. Jeanne cranked up the volume a notch, handing the CD box to Rosa, who suddenly felt like Poland in the path of Germany.

I am so alone, so alo-one,
All alone, far from you.
Do you miss me?
Cos I miss you.
I'm all alone, all at sea.

I am so alone, so alo-one,
All alone, that's what I am.
Without you my love,
There's no blue sky above.
I'm all alone, all at sea.

And on and on it went. Rosa looked down at the black and white photo of a tall, thin man who strangely enough reminded her of Mayor Duressac, the only difference being that poor Renard had a face as long as a fiddle. His horse-like teeth gleamed like an oversized pearl necklace. She found him immediately, irredeemably unhappy.

Fortunately, all things must come to an end, and so it was with the song. Jeanne cleared her throat:

"So?"

"So...?" Rosa countered.

"I wanna know what you think!"

"What I think... Does it really matter what I think?"

The other three girls looked at her and rubbed their eyes. Heather tried her best to hide a smile behind her hand.

"Surely you can't deny, oh little Miss Culture, that this song is simply the most touching thing you've ever heard! Are you going to tell us that Renard is a failure?

Five million albums sold in France. Five million! They'd never seen the like of it! And now he lives in Paris, a real poet for the ages! His songs are played all over France. He's on every television channel, every show is sold out across the country."

Rosa's top lip quivered as though a fish hook had caught in it. She could feel words welling up inside her, words she could no longer contain. It had never happened to her before. She had the unpleasant sensation that she was about to vomit. She searched every eye that was trained on her for a way to stop the words from coming, but she could feel her mouth opening. The words spewed out onto the floor of Jeanne Joyal's parlour like cow dung onto a flower-covered meadow in June:

"Poor France!"

Jeanne Joyal took a deep breath. Heather, Perdita, and Jacqueline had stopped breathing long ago. A yawning Siberian silence settled over the Joyal boarding house. Jeanne very deliberately turned off the music, closed the armoire, and left the room. They heard her slam the door to her room at the end of the hall. The four young women gaped at each other in astonishment. Rosa felt a fertile seed begin to expand in her pelvic region. Her nipples hardened, making her blush. She felt not unlike an inebriated Saint Bernadette Soubirous, tottering to her feet in the middle of the Sunday homily to declare: "Is anyone else feeling a little frisky this morning? I could use a little *action* here!"

Then it happened.

The kind of laugh that leaves you bent double.

It tickled the back of the Ontarian's throat, rounded the Haitian lips, then shook all of Guruistan. The laughter was blind to geography. It fed off its own guffaws, taking sustenance from the tears that streamed down the women's faces. The aftershocks were felt for a solid hour. For that short period of time when the laughter rang out, Rosa felt perfectly attuned to the Self. For as long as they echoed around her, the fits of laughter managed to fill the gulf that had formed between the cool, windy place where her soul longed to be and the hot, humid city where duty was holding her body. For as long as she laughed, it occurred to her that she was happy where she was and wanted to stay there.

Rosa had to leave for work. Thinking back on the evening's hilarity, she had to suppress a giggle as she rode the number 55 bus to the hotel, while the three other gigglers buried their faces in their pillows, worried they might wake the neighbours. Sleep was in short supply that night at 8510 Rue du Saint-Ciboire.

Rosa was still clutching her sides when she started her shift. The laughter would return with epileptic force as soon as she thought of anything but the image of her dead mother lying in her casket, the only tactic she had found to stop people thinking she had completely lost her mind. As she consulted the ledger that Sri had filled with his round handwriting, she was surprised to see that Mr. and Mrs. Smith were already in Room 21, while the Durands had taken number 23. It was an early start for a Monday night. At 3:30 a.m., she made the camomile tea that Jasmine and her dancers were in the habit of taking with her before bed, all except for Carlota, who insisted on mint tea every night. Rosa, like every young communist, was very fond of camomile.

Lenin's Great-Granddaughters almost choked on their camomile flowers when Rosa told them what had happened on Saint-Ciboire. She couldn't have said why exactly, but she threw in the odd detail that, while not strictly coming under the category of fabrication, made the anecdote all the more memorable. Nelly and Blondie, the two German strippers who'd never understood why Rosa had agreed to live with such an unpleasant individual in the first place, lapped up Rosa's impression of Renard.

"I vood haff paid a lott to tsee zat!" Blondie said in her fine German accent.

The women complimented Rosa on her new sweater before heading up to the third floor for the night. In Room 22, Ludmilla removed her makeup as she chatted to Tatiana, who was sprawled on the bed flicking through the *Étoile de Montréal*, a daily newspaper renowned for its well-measured positions on the potentially explosive issues of the day. It was all the reading that Tatiana had the strength for at that late hour and, as luck would have it, the only newspaper the Butler Motor Hotel subscribed to.

"Listen to this, Ludmilla Ilinichna Vladimirova! The Arts & Entertainment section has a review of our show. There's even a photo of Jasmine."

"Well, read on, won't you, Tatiana Andreïevna Bakoulina! I can't wait to hear it."

"This spectacle is degrading to even the tables and chairs forced to endure it, according far too much intelligence to what amounts to no more than a striptease. Spare us the pseudo-communist iconography! Let's not beat about the bush: Lenin's Great-Granddaughters are just a pitiful excuse to further exploit women's bodies. Frankly, this sad call for help does not transcend the art."

"That's a good one. The *Étoile de Montréal* is one to talk about intelligence. It reminds me of the time I went out with an opera singer back in Saint Petersburg and he wouldn't stop going on about nuclear physics. Since when have you read the newspaper reviews, my dear friend? Wasn't it you who was telling me just yesterday that this country doesn't know the first thing about art?"

"And I stand by that, Tatiana Andreïevna Bakoulina."

As she did every night, Ludmilla had brought the cups up to the room she shared with Tatiana. She insisted on washing them herself. "I don't want you to have to wash up on top of everything else," she told Rosa in a motherly tone. "You're not a servant to the tsarina, after all." Ludmilla conscientiously washed every last cup in the bathroom sink, amusing herself as she did by reading her eleven comrades' futures at the bottom of each. An honours graduate of an underground college for clairvoyance in Saint Petersburg, Ludmilla was reminded by this simple exercise of her teenage years on the banks of the Neva, where she would often spend her evenings watching the bridges raised to allow the boats through. She always kept her prophecies to herself, unless they involved Shu-Misty's cup, easily identified by the shade of the Chinese girl's red lipstick. Ludmilla had been trying for weeks to win Shu-Misty's affections, without drawing the attention of the others so as not to cause undue tension in the workplace. She was sure Shu-Misty would notice she had become the centre of a spiral of concupiscence. But Shu-Misty couldn't have cared less. She was secretly in love with Carlota, whose preference for mint reminded her of a contortion instructor who had been her first sapphic lover at the Shanghai Circus School. She was nothing if not well-mannered, though, and accepted Ludmilla's prophecies, while dreaming they were addressed to her in a Caribbean accent. Picking up one of the cups that evening, Ludmilla let out a horrified, throaty shriek and dropped the cup to the bathroom floor, where it smashed into smithereens.

"What are you wailing about like a Cossack?" demanded Tatiana, who was trimming her toenails beside her bed.

Ludmilla emerged from the bathroom, the colour completely drained from her face.

"What on earth did you see, Ludmilla Ilinichna Vladimirova?" Tatiana insisted. "Why that awful screaming?"

"It's HIM. It's Him, Tatiana Andreïevna Bakoulina! He's back!"

"Who's back? Did you just see Comrade Stalin's face looking up at you from the bottom of the toilet bowl?"

"It's worse than that. It's Him."

"All right, calm down. Come here, Ludmilla Ilinichna Vladimirova, and tell me everything."

"It was at the bottom of Rosa's cup."

"How can you be so sure? It's not as if the cups have names on them, and they all look alike."

"It's the only one without lipstick on the rim. She never wears makeup. It's her, Tatiana Andreïevna Bakoulina! Oh, the poor thing! That unfortunate child! I must stop it. He's so close to her. She doesn't suspect a thing."

"Oh, stop snivelling!"

Ludmilla was slapped a first time. With the front of the hand.

"Forgive me! I shouldn't have done that. Let me give you a hug. Listen to me, Ludmilla Ilinichna Vladimirova. Do you remember what you read in your tarot cards back when we were sixteen and in Saint Petersburg? My friend, the wonderful Nikolaï Koulinov Raskalchov was to become secretary of the Communist Party. You were absolutely sure of it. And do you know what Nikolaï Koulinov Raskalchov does for a living now? He steals BMWs in Berlin. And the party? Do you know what's become of the party? It's a social club for retirees!"

"Tatiana Andreïevna Bakoulina, that wasn't the same thing. That was tarot. I was hopeless at tarot! The cards showed him behind the wheel of a fancy car just like Khrushchev's. So, I was sure it meant he would be called on to lead the party. I didn't so much as glance at the next card. I got it all wrong. But this, this is tea leaves! I was top of my class in reading tea leaves. I called the collapse of the Soviet Union before the Berlin Wall fell. Even my teachers would ask my advice. Oh, Tatiana Andreïevna

Bakoulina, my dear Tatiana Andreïevna Bakoulina, what are we going to do? We have to help her!"

Ludmilla was slapped a second time. With the front and back of the hand.

"You'll do no such thing, you little idiot! It's just tiredness talking. Don't you go scaring the poor girl with your two-bit fortune telling. You'll only terrify her, and you know perfectly well that the very last thing she needs right now is to be afraid. You say it yourself every time: 'If it's in the tea, it's plain to see! If it's in the cup, it's coming up!' It's herbal tea, not real tea, for a start! Do you read herbal tea leaves, too?"

"You're right, Tatiana Andreïevna Bakoulina. I am but a messenger for the other world. I can't alter the future any more than you can swap the last page of a book for another because you don't like the ending."

"Just as well. Otherwise that would be the end for Russian literature!"

"And French cinema."

"OK. You're calmer now, I see. Go to sleep, Ludmilla Ilinichna Vladimirova... Nightie-night!"

What Ludmilla didn't say was that she could read herbal tea leaves every bit as well as real tea, perhaps even better. She finished sweeping up the teacup shards, took a long bath in scalding-hot water until her fingers and toes bloomed like cauliflowers, and lay down on her double bed. She sobbed in silence so as not to wake Tatiana, who would only have slapped her a third time: once with the front of her hand, then the back, then the front again. She didn't fall asleep until noon.

In the hotel lobby, Gillian, the Butler blowhard, was in and out of the hotel like there was no tomorrow. "Can't talk, darling: farmers' convention tonight! It's go, go, go! The knees are scraped off me," Gillian joked as she walked past the front desk, where Rosa was engrossed in her sums, and dashed back out to Boulevard Saint-Laurent.

Alone again, Rosa stood behind the desk, struggling to get the credit and debit columns to balance, and trying not to think back to the evening that had been cut short at Jeanne Joyal's. She could feel a sleepy yawn coming on, and went off to pour herself a cup of filter coffee in the office. She didn't even hear the lobby door open as a uniformed man stepped inside and sauntered over to the counter. By the time she looked up, it was already too late.

That Tuesday, November 14, 2000, at 5:25 a.m., what wasn't to happen happened: Constable Réjean Savoie, who had been with station 21 ever since joining the Montreal police department, walked into the Butler Motor Hotel and, with that, into Rosa Ost's life. Our little Gaspé girl, so proud at having worked out, without any help from Cassandra, the hotel's profit margins on a weekly, monthly, and annual basis, looked up to see a policeman's cap towering over her by a good head and a half. Her red pen rolled across the counter and fell at Officer Savoie's feet. Gallant police officer that he was, he stooped down to pick it up. He took off his cap with his right hand and ran the fingers of his left through the short red hair that fell and rose again as Rosa stared. For the duration of that second that lasted a full fifty centuries, Rosa heard a voice rising within her, a voice she had never heard before. She knew the words. It was Marx, only it was Marx read aloud in a warm, manly voice, the voice that Mayor Duressac would sometimes use to whisper into Terese Ost's ear as she told him to mind himself because Rosa was nearby. The voice reminded her of the Conservative MPs' groans of desire as they watched Jasmine dance at the Nile. The voice grabbed her... *down there*. The voice... his voice. His hair shone an indecent albeit natural red that was nonetheless illusory, impossible, revolutionary in the Bolshevik sense of the term. And the voice rang in Rosa's ears: "All the rays of light in their original composition are reflected by silver, while red alone, the colour of the highest potency, is reflected by gold." That same piece about gold and precious metals.

Savoie grinned. His teeth, two perfect rows of rare pearls from the southern seas, parted to reveal a little pink tongue with a rounded tip. Catching sight of the tongue as it darted around the police officer's mouth, Rosa felt an inexplicable urge to slide her heels a few centimetres apart as she stood behind her desk. The colour Red had spoken. It was the beginning and the end of everything.

"Evening, miss. Officer Savoie from the Montreal police department, station 21. Sorry to bother you at work. I was thinking you'd likely be able to help me tonight."

How is it that when it comes to affairs of the heart, supply often creates demand? It wasn't as though Rosa was looking to settle down. After all, her existence boiled down to working nights at the Butler, taking the 55 out to

Villeray, and scouring the city for a way to rouse the west wind. She hadn't asked anything of Cupid. This wasn't the first time Rosa's heart had been in demand in the love economy, but she'd always either ignored or declined such solicitations. Why rush to fritter away all the affection allocated to us at birth? Why hurry to squander the treasure we so desperately seek twenty years later?

The officer's Acadian accent immediately caught Rosa in its clutches. Might it have been the pure, crystal-clear *d* sounds, the lack of a *z* inserted before every *i*, that cut Rosa's IQ by half? Might it have been the sing-song New Brunswick voice, of which she knew only the *Pélagie-la-Charrette* recordings Terese would listen to as she peeled her potatoes? Might it have been the athletic figure the police officer cut as he hooked his left thumb in his pants pocket, as though he'd just bumped into an old friend? Or was it the blue uniform that clung to his muscles, the muscles of an Olympic wrestler?

And what about those blue eyes! Blue as the Gulf of St. Lawrence in October. Blue as one thousand promises of happiness. Blue as the sound of wedding bells. Blue on a face so fair as to set a French queen dreaming. And freckles... everywhere. Each one propelled from its base like a Soviet missile, exploding over Rosa's flawless skin and bringing it to a boil. Tiny wrinkles tugging at his eyes. Six marks of wisdom. How old could this street-car named Desire possibly be? Forty? Forty-five? It was impossible to tell. Men over forty who work out tend to defy all attempts to pin down their age. Rosa gritted her teeth, her hand still clutching her boiling-hot cup of coffee. That I-Want-You Red began to blossom again in her quivering lips.

"My sergeant—he's outside in the car—suspects two prostitutes from Sainte-Catherine of meeting their clients in your hotel. You wouldn't have seen them go by, by any chance?"

He produced a photo of Cassandra and Gillian from his shirt pocket. They were standing on the sidewalk, smoking long cigarettes. Rosa muttered something unintelligible.

"I'm sorry, miss. Didn't catch that, I'm afraid."

"Red! Ggolour of the highest potency!" she cried.

She was losing control. She could feel her toes curl, her nipples harden. She felt like an idiot—and proud of it.

"I'm sorry. I don't follow you at all. Red? What red?"

Rosa caught only half of Savoie's reply. Her hand suddenly jolted in a nervous twitch, flinging her full cup of piping-hot coffee all over the constable's chest.

Officer Savoie let out a painful "Ahhh!" his big blue eyes growing wide, then grabbed both sides of his buttoned-down shirt and ripped it open in one swift movement, revealing a smooth, hairless chest, reddened by the coffee, that was straight out of an American gay porn movie.

"Bejeezuz!" Savoie yelped in pain. "Watch it!"

He hopped from one foot to the other, as Rosa beat both fists on the counter, shouting, "Yes! Yes! Yes!"

When she returned to her senses, the police officer was dabbing at the drops of coffee that had pearled on his taut nipples.

"Oh! Sir. I'm... I'm so sorry. I didn't mean to. Did I... did I sggald you? I'm such a gglutz."

Rosa held her head in her hands. Her accent had come back with a vengeance.

"Oh! It's nothing, miss. That's one way to make an impression, though. Did you... did you just say gglutz?"

"Yes! I mean klutz! Klutz! Peter Piper picked a pot of pickled peppers! There!"

"You're from the Gaspé Peninsula? I recognize your accent. I know that part of the world. You're practically Acadians yourselves, with all those Landrys, Leblancs, and Boudreaus. My brother lives in New Richmond! His kids can't pronounce the *k* sound to save their lives. Don't get me wrong, I love it. We Acadians all have family somewhere in the Gaspé. And those Chic-Choc mountains of yours are incredible."

"Oh, they're just as much yours as they are mine."

Rosa no longer knew what she thought was incredible or not. She no longer knew very much at all, to be honest. The feeling of empty-headedness was new to her, and quite pleasant really. The man's Acadian dialect had burrowed its way into the yawning chasm in which Rosa could now feel great clumps of the stuff forming—the very opposite of Boredom. While the police officer put his coffee-stained shirt back on, she struggled to recall the first thing about herself. For example, had someone at that very moment asked her what her name was, she would have hesitated before an impressive array of possibilities. She decided to test herself with a tricky question: What's the capital of Cuba? She looked Savoie in the eye and asked him the same question.

"Cuba? Cuba? Uh, let me think... Aha, it's Havana!" he said, buttoning up his shirt.

"Of ggourse it is. What an idiot I am. You're so gglever. I'm sure you were top of your gglass. Tee hee!"

The officer blushed, which didn't help matters. He let out an embarrassed "Pfff" as he did up his collar.

"Everyone knows that," he said shyly.

Havana. Talk turned to Havana that morning in the Butler lobby. The Havana they'd never been to, but would surely visit one day. It was Savoie's turn to lose half his brain cells.

"Cuba... si... si... si..."

It was a childhood dream. It was written in the sky in flaming letters. They would walk the streets and wander beneath the arches of the presidential palace.

"Ah, Fidel. Faithful Fidel. I'd be faithful, that's for sure... Oh, you mean Castro! Fidel Castro! I misunderstood, miss. I... uh... Of course, he's a great dictator. I mean, uh... they don't make dictators like him anymore. Saddam can't hold a candle to him with his weapons of mass seduction... Uh... Let me take *your* shirt off for you. Uh, I mean..."

The poor Acadian made one slip after another. Soon he was nothing but a red lobster in uniform. Silence descended over them. A car horn blared. Once. Twice. Three times. A fog horn warning ships they might be in danger of colliding with a reef on their nighttime journey. The *S.S. Savoie* and the *H.M.S. Ost* were on course for a maritime disaster in the dark of night. A voice. A car horn. The fog horn turned out to be Sergeant Cayouette,

121

yelling at his colleague to get out of the hotel. That they didn't have all night. To get his Acadian ass in gear. Savoie left without a word, like a dog responding to a whistle, a certain elegant swing to his gait.

Rosa stood there behind her front desk, feeling as though she had just found and lost something or someone that she had long been looking for. She quickly banished from her mind the voices telling her Savoie was much too old for her.

The police car didn't budge from outside the main door to the hotel. Rosa's thoughts turned to Gillian, who had gone up to Room 21 fifteen minutes earlier. She would be coming back down any second now, and was sure to come face to face with Sergeant Cayouette and Officer Savoie. The phone. Punch in 9. 21. "Gillian, stay right where you are. The cops are outside!"

Where do these reflexes come from, those reflexes that drag us down a dangerous slope without us even realizing it? Between Montreal's force of law and order and the world's oldest profession, our little Rosa had just chosen her side. Would her slippery descent into the vortex of depravity meet with a happy end? Only a Saint Petersburg stripper or a Notre-Dame-du-Cachalot winkle could say for sure.

The police eventually left. Rosa called again to say she could come back down. The lawbreaker, unintimidated by the cops and keen not to interrupt a night that was on course to be a profitable one, thanked Rosa for her act of feminine solidarity by slapping a U.S. hundred-dollar bill down in front of her. "That, honey, is for what you just did. You really are a good'un." Then she headed back out to her November sidewalk. Rosa stared at the green bill, her mouth hanging open. The wool of her new sweater suddenly burned hot on her neck. On the white ceiling, two nocturnal insects, well used to seeing Rosa struggle to balance the books at seven in the morning, hadn't missed a thing. "Can cockroaches talk?" To that particular burning question, Rosa would be able to reply, the very next day, "Yes, but only to settle a particularly thorny moral dilemma, which these days is rare." Catching sight of the creepy critters, a shiver ran down her spine. Cockroaches, just like hundreds of other repugnant bugs, tend to prefer the big city to the Gaspé Peninsula. And young Gaspesians whose fate leads them to the big smoke begin their urban existence in student hovels. One can well imagine the squeal of an eighteen-year-old Gaspé girl from Cap-Chat or Percé who, on the very night she moves to Montreal, realizes she'll now be sharing her life with those creatures from hell. A Montrealer the same age might mumble something to the effect of "Oh shoot, a cockroach." But the girl from the Gaspé will let out an eight-minute scream in B major before calling her mom back home. Poor Rosa! We know she found them disgusting little creatures because, upon catching sight of them, she exclaimed: "Ggoggroaches. Gross!" She took an aerosol can of some German chemical concoction from her desk drawer and sprayed a generous stream over the horrible little things. It was in that toxic cloud that Carlota and Roberta found Rosa half out of her mind.

"Whatever's the matter, my little garden Rose?"

The garden Rose in question was surprised to see the two Cubans back at the Butler so early. They had mentioned something about a sudden onset of insomnia driving them from their room to go for a walk through the city streets, only to find themselves plunged headfirst in a moral quandary they thought they'd left behind on leaving their native island. Rosa told them the source of the banknote that was still sitting on the front desk like an unsolved problem. She explained she was reluctant to take it, given the questionable circumstances that had led to it landing there. Carlota and Roberta understood their friend's inner turmoil, even though, truth be told, they secretly found her preoccupations rather childish. While they might not have been involved in Gillian and Cassandra's criminal activities, the two dancers weren't in the least disgusted by them. For the two tropical birds from the south, the very idea of giving up dancing to walk the streets all night left them shaking their heads. In Lenin's Great-Granddaughters they'd found a steady revenue stream, an outlet for their creative impulses, and, more importantly, a family, all things that were foreign to Gillian and Cassandra. Carlota could sense Rosa's growing sense of helplessness.

"Why not just pick it up and put it in your wallet?"

"Oh, I don't know. It feels like I'd be compromising myself. Mom wouldn't have liked that."

"Come on now, Rosa! It's not like you had to get down on your knees to earn that money. Gillian paid you for passing along information. Your crime isn't prostitution, it's obstructing the work of a police officer, and who can blame you? You could always say you didn't know what Gillian was up to."

"But that's the thing. At that point, I knew exactly what she was doing."

"So, why did you keep Gillian away from that cop then?"

"I'm not sure, Carlota. I didn't want to see that happen."

"So, you made a choice."

"Yeah, but I didn't put a monetary value on that choice. I acted as a friend, then she turns around and treats me like I'm some sort of informer."

Carlota couldn't believe her ears.

"Let me get this straight. It's more the fact she paid you for what you did. That's what's leaving a bad taste in your mouth. Not the act itself."

"I think so. I think that's it."

Carlota placed her right hand on Rosa's left shoulder and declared:

"Blessed are those who still believe that money isn't the answer to every problem."

Roberta didn't say a thing. The discomfort she felt was becoming more and more palpable. At last she decided to speak up.

"Carlota, do you really believe that? Do you really think that things are so simple?"

Carlota shot her compatriot a look. She was getting on her nerves, always trying to contradict her.

"So, you'd like Rosa to hand the money back to Gillian and say, 'I can't accept this. I have zero respect for your

125

work and everything it represents.' Is that what you want?"

"No, Carlota, what I'm saying is, I can see where Rosa's coming from. And you of all people should understand her..."

"I'm not a huge fan of your dot-dot-dots, Roberta. What are you implying?"

"You know exactly what I mean, Carlota Margarita Hernández! Let's just say that Gillian and Cassandra's line of work isn't entirely unknown to you."

Carlota balled her fists, then turned and climbed the staircase that led to her room. She'd had enough of the debate, by the look of things. Rosa plucked up the courage to inquire further about the three little dots, and Roberta didn't need asking twice. Until the previous year, Carlota had been a chambermaid in a three-star hotel in Cuba where Canadian retirees would spend their winters. All of them men. Thanks to generous pension plans and advances in pharmacology, the ex-manual labourers, ex-lawyers, ex-policemen, and ex-accountants had all been guaranteed a second youth in the sun to go with their rock-hard erections. Carlota had managed to sink her claws into a former police sergeant from Quebec, giving herself up to pleasures that women in the north considered too degrading, in exchange for a handful of green bills similar in all respects to the one sitting on Rosa's counter. Believing Carlota to be an honest woman, the sergeant had married her and brought her home to Canada, to some godforsaken village whose name Roberta had now forgotten. "Somewhere the middle of nowhere," she told Rosa. "Near where you're from." But two weeks after the newlyweds returned to Canada, the sergeant had been found dead, having eaten a contaminated mussel at a family get-together. Nobody had ever been able to pin it on the Cuban, since she'd eaten the mussels herself. Rosa conceded:

"He must've been from Rimouski. They know all kinds of things there, but they can't tell if a mussel's contaminated or not. They'd never admit it, though. It's their Achilles heel."

"Well, Carlota knows exactly what one looks like... if you catch my drift... She used to be an engineer at the seafood-processing plant in Varadero before she became a chambermaid. She's always had a nose for a good thing, if you ask me..."

Roberta's little dots spoke volumes. Rosa couldn't believe it. A murderer! There was a murderer staying at her hotel!

"So, just you listen to me, honey," Roberta continued. "Carlota came to Montreal and auditioned with me for the troupe. Jasmine took her on right away. She inherited the cop's pension and all his money. But there's no reason to be jealous about it: she shares what she has! Every time we're accused of gross indecency and Jasmine has to appear in court, it's Carlota who pays the lawyer. We all profit from what she did. So, don't you worry your little head about that hundred-dollar bill. Just as long as you use it to help those around you, nobody's gonna mind where the money came from. It's people we should be judging, not bank notes."

Feeling a little better, Rosa pocketed the bill. *In God We Trust*. She thanked Roberta for her precious advice, promising not to breathe a word about Carlota's dark past.

"Hey, I have a proverb for you. I know you like them. It's in Spanish, so listen carefully. *No hay mal que dure cien años ni cuerpo que lo resista.*"

"What does it mean?"

"It means... uh... it means nothing lasts forever. This too will pass. Literally, it means no ill will lasts one hundred years, and even if it does last a hundred years, no body is made to endure it. In other words, we'll be free of all evil before a hundred years are up. Just as well, eh? *¿Verdad?*"

Roberta followed her compatriot upstairs to bed.

::

After her nights as receptionist and controller at the Butler Motor Hotel, Rosa would sometimes walk the length of Boulevard Saint-Laurent all the way to Villeray. The aim of her long morning walk, which took her an hour and a quarter, was to tire out her little legs and ensure a dreamless sleep that day. Passing by the Saint-Laurent metro station and its collection of lost souls on her right, she would ignore the rumbling of the number 55 bus that would normally have dropped her off at the corner of Jarry twenty minutes later. Instead, she would stride purposefully up Saint-Laurent, crossing Sherbrooke and, wide-eyed as ever, continue along the street that over the years had become a swarming, bustling museum of every luxury and hardship, every language and colour, every sorrow and enchantment. Rosa would absorb every detail of Boulevard Saint-Laurent, her eyes like Champollion's deciphering the dust-covered inscriptions of the Rosetta Stone. She would cast a glacial glance at the grey monolith that was the Ex-Centris cinema, then cross the street just to get a closer look at Schwartz's, the world's greasiest greasy spoon, which had managed through sheer perseverance to elevate its kosher beef grease to the rank of national institution. Just past Duluth, in the relative still of early morning, she would admire the fabric merchants' window displays, imagining that an American doctor had managed to cure Aunt Zenaida of the colour blindness that painted everything in her sights mauve, violet, or lilac, and that the elderly seamstress would discover with her adoptive granddaughter the reassuring patterns and hues of the seas of textiles. On the far side of Mont-Royal, Rosa would always rummage in her pocket and deposit in a grimy hand—connected by a skeletal bone to a scrawny, intoxicated body—a glistening coin that would fall like a droplet of water onto the burning-hot stone of hard times. *LUNETTERIE NEW LOOK!* Saint-Joseph! Then a string of evocatively named Indian restaurants before Rosa made her way under the railroad bridge. *MILLION TAPIS ET TUILES.* Who would ever need a million rugs? Maybe the up-and-coming young executives surely condemned to eternal damnation, having had no qualms about moving into one of the condos in what had once been the church of Saint-

Zotique and was now, much to the archbishops' dismay, an apartment block. Rosa loved it.

The young Marxist then went on a journey to Mussolini's homeland. Milano: Italian charcuterie. Faema: espresso machines. *CAMMINA... CAMMINA... CHI CALZA CORTINA*. It sounded like opera. Humming along to a Puccini aria, Rosa made up a melody to accompany the Italian words she didn't understand, to help her on her way. A *donna*, her surname ending on a vowel, passed by, heard the little song, and smiled. She didn't have the heart to tell our little Rosa that she'd just ended the *Tosca* finale with a slogan for Italian pantyhose: *The lady who wears Cortina pantyhose will walk and walk*. And walk Rosa did, through the stagnant November air that the wind refused to stir.

Singing as she walked was one of the odd little habits Rosa had picked up from Terese and the women of Notre-Dame-du-Cachalot. GLUM had ensured that the collectivist mindset of the peninsula's inhabitants wouldn't be polluted by modern-day radio or television waves. Rosa and her ilk had therefore been deprived of the somewhat uneven radio programming and the TV variety shows that were otherwise freely available to the good people of French Canada. Instead the villagers had to make do with the records and cassettes that Mayor Duressac would order once a year by phone from a department store in Rimouski: "And send us another of Chopin's *Noggturnes*, would you? I'm afraid Mrs. Starfiche sggratched the last ggopy we had..." Jazz, folk, classical, French *chansonniers*, world beats, cabaret, Kurt Weill and Barbara, sambas and arias—those were the sounds heard in the homes of Notre-Dame-du-Cachalot. Their heads full of songs and melodies, the women would clean their huge windows as they sung *Vissi d'arte*, while the men gutted herrings and smelt as they belted out Piaf and Brassens. The songs would fill the silence, covering the sound of the waves as they washed up on the grey shingles and the wind as it howled through the eaves. There was no shame in walking through the village belting out Gilles Vigneault at the top of one's lungs, quite the opposite. The villagers carried the songs around with them as others do rosary beads. And there was no reason for Rosa to turn her back on the custom of the country just because she was now living in the city. After all, wasn't the silence of that November morning in Villeray every bit as imposing as the stillness of the Gaspé Peninsula? Wasn't it worth filling with a song, even if it was altogether lacking in good taste?

Rosa proved she could be just as much of a Montrealer as the next person by crossing Jean-Talon on a red light, with not a look to her left or right. Jarry Park, the lungs of Villeray. North of Jean-Talon, Saint-Laurent was no longer one way and the boulevard was lined on either side by a string of depressing, red-brick buildings. There was a twenty-four-hour gym frequented by men and women for whom any time was a good time for muscle-building. Behind the plate glass windows, men glistened with sweat in their sports apparel as they jogged on treadmills, their eyes trained on an imaginary horizon. Rosa made a habit of stopping before the five

Roman gods with their dark curly hair, echoes from lost Pompei, virile dreamboats, gifts from Calabria and Sicily, burning off the dreaded fat that threatened to overcome their proud abs. She stood on the sidewalk, separated from the mass of muscles by nothing more than a pane of glass. They ran in her direction but never reached her, those stationary, breathless men who looked out curiously at the early-morning passerby. No one could accuse the young woman of ogling, nor of brazenly stoking the fires of her desires with the sight of their perfect bodies. She was simply fascinated by the men's synchronized steps, which, had it not been for the treadmills, would have left them bloody-nosed against the glass, like sparrows crashing into the windows of a skyscraper. Only Officer Savoie could reach her, and he didn't even need to run. A few words would be enough to leave Rosa in a state of catatonic hypnosis. Rosa often gave the runners a smile, which they unfailingly answered with a wink that momentarily concealed one handsome chestnut or brown iris. A little further on, she'd turn right onto Jarry to arrive, a few blocks after that, at Rue du Saint-Ciboire, where she'd find her landlady in a gardening frenzy. On this particular morning, Jeanne was busy raking up the orange and red maple leaves from the lawn in front of her house.

"Rosa! Have you seen all these friggin' leaves? I picked up just as many not three days ago. Goddamn tree! I wanted to cut it down, but the pen-pushers at City Hall refused. Well, they're not the ones that have to rake up all the leaves, are they? They get to sit on their fat asses, raking in our tax dollars instead. Hold the bag for a sec while I fill it, would you, sweetie?"

Rosa would rather have been heading to bed for a little shut-eye, but when a Gaspé girl's asked to help, she just can't say no. Jeanne went on cursing the bureaucrats who not only forced her to clear the snow off the sidewalk in front of her home, but insisted she use orange garbage bags for the leaves, too.

"What the hell difference does it make to them if I stick 'em in green bags or orange ones?"

"I think it's because they compost them and the orange bags help them find the leaves quickly."

"Compost my leaves?"

"Yeah, for flowers and trees in the city parks."

"You mean to say that leaves from *my* maple tree that *I* bought with *my* money are saving *the City* money, all while they don't think twice about hiking up *my* property taxes?"

Rosa decided to try out her new Spanish proverb on Jeanne. The landlady looked her square in the eye and advised her not to believe everything those foreigners went around telling her. No pain lasts a hundred years? What about the English occupation? It'd been going on since 1760! The Spanish proverb was dismissed as a steaming pile of B.S. The two women fell quiet as they worked. Rosa was perplexed. Judging by the maple tree's girth, it must've been more than fifty years old. Had Jeanne planted it when she was still a child? And where did she come from anyway? Had she always lived there? The question was brushed aside by an astral event. For the first time in that grey month of November, the still-low sun peeked between two clouds and fell on Jeanne Joyal, covering the fall scene with its feeble rays. Rosa noticed that her shadow stretched halfway across the street. Her head elongated by the laws of physics, her strangely long and lanky body, her thin black arms on the paved road, covered in early-morning frost, as they held the bag that Jeanne was filling with leaves. The image of the two of them at work gladdened the young woman's heart. She looked for Jeanne's shadow to the right of hers. She didn't see it. Her gaze returned to the spot where the black silhouette should have been. Nothing. She dropped the bag of leaves and rubbed her eyes. Twice. Still not a thing.

Jeanne Joyal had no shadow.

Pleased with her handiwork, Jeanne put her rake and shovel back in the shed and thanked her young boarder, who was still dumbfounded by what she'd just discovered. Jeanne climbed into her van, ready to head out inspecting for the Office québécois de la langue française. Rosa, meanwhile, staggered zombie-like to her room. She lay on her bed, but couldn't fall asleep. Had it been an illusion? Had the past few weeks exhausted her to the point that she could no longer make out a person's shadow on the pavement? No. She'd seen what she'd seen and would spend the rest of her life questioning the strange absence. Perdita had just gotten up and was quietly getting ready to leave for her university classes. Rosa couldn't resist.

"Perdita?"

"Yes, Rosa. You're not asleep?"

"No, I can't fall asleep, Perdita."

"How come?"

"Sit down. Come sit on your bed, Perdita. I need to talk to you. Just listen!"

"You're so tense, my little Rosa. You look like the stiff, cold body of my grandmother, lying on a bed of daisies in her tomb."

"Believe me, Perdita, I almost envy your grandmother. Can you promise you won't breathe a word of what I'm about to tell you, my friend? My sidekick? My roommate?"

"Spit it out, Rosa! Don't tell me some man was disrespectful to you at work? If he was, I'd only be forced to tell you how you Western girls really go around asking for it!"

"It's not that. I've just come in from outside. I was helping Jeanne rake up the last of the leaves before the snow comes. We were both there, just in front of the steps in the sun."

"It's true we haven't seen much of the sun these days. It reminds me of the time my cousin and I took the train to Zîb for the winter cabbage festival. Even the good people of Zîb were surprised to see the sun in November."

"It's not the sun that surprised me, Perdita."

"What? Did Jeanne not say a word for five minutes? She didn't treat you to a demonstration of how Quebecers traditionally rake up the leaves?"

"Enough with the sarcasm! At this time of year, we should all cast a long shadow, right?"

"It's an astronomic fact."

"Well, get this: Jeanne doesn't have a shadow."

Perdita froze, then grabbed her roommate by the shoulders.

"Can you...? Can you say that again?"

"Jeanne Joyal doesn't have a shadow."

"But you know what that means?"

"No. All I know is it's not normal."

Perdita shrieked and crumpled to the floor.

"Rosa, Rosa, swear you're telling me the truth. Are you absolutely sure you didn't see a shadow at Jeanne's feet? Tell me you're making it up!"

"I swear it's the truth. I had a good look. The sun's rays pass through her like glass."

A second shriek, just as long as the first, emanated from the pile of rags that the poor girl from Guruistan had become.

"So, that's it. It's happening. Ohh, I should have seen it coming!"

"Geez Perdita. Have you lost your mind?"

"You don't get it, Rosa. The prophecies of Shah Gidogstori couldn't be clearer."

"I... You're gonna have to refresh my memory about Shah Gidogstori's prophecies."

"Don't you learn anything at school in this country? Shah Gidogstori! Grandfather to the Great Guru! Prophecy Number Four. Think, Rosa, think!"

"I swear I have no idea what you're going on about."

"Rosa, listen. The sacred texts are very clear:

Yellow pestilence in a land so cold
Of the eighth month two thousand years old
Will see demented lady of the French
Stop not the sun and cause a wrench"

"A wrench?"

"Yes. The unspeakable!"

"What on earth are you jabbering on about?"

"Listen to me: *all* of Shah Gidogstori's prophecies have come true, every single one of them. The bubonic plague, Attila the Hun, Napoleon, Hitler, Hiroshima, Thatcher! And now... this! This explains everything. It's her, Rosa!"

"Look, Perdita. Everything you just reeled off, it's all well and good, but it could mean any old thing! The demented lady might even be you."

"Oh really? And what do you say to this? Just give me a sec while I find it... quatrain number forty-four."

Rosa sighed.

"Here it is:

For so long lost to all of time
Did not burn, spared by the Swine
The demented lady shall seek the wind
In land of new Gaul chagrined"

"Well, you took the words right out of my mouth."

"Laugh! Laugh away, you heathen! You'll be bowing down before me soon enough, but it'll be too late by then."

"That's just it, Perdita. It's late. I need to go to sleep now. Can we talk more about the demented lady some other time?"

Perdita blew her nose noisily. It was time for her integral calculus class. Rosa was left perplexed and exhausted, feeling so helpless that her body had told her thoughts to pipe down and mind their own business. It wouldn't be uncommon for a wife whose husband has just announced that he's leaving for Arizona with his pert little blonde secretary to react by lying down for a little nap. And that's exactly the kind of sleep that Rosa fell into. By the time she woke up, Perdita was back home and sitting at her desk, chipping away at an equation that had been bugging her for weeks.

CHAPTER 4

Nostalgia isn't what it used to be

TUESDAY EVENINGS at Jeanne Joyal's were given over to readings of Quebec literature. After supper, the boarders would take their places in the parlour, which Jeanne had transformed into a reading circle for the occasion. Tea was served. Table lamps would be lit, and reading glasses donned. Every week for the past four weeks, the girls had sat in a circle and listened to Jeanne reading from a thick volume she was especially fond of. While these evenings meant they had nothing to do but sit back and listen to Jeanne read from a historical novel, there was always the risk of falling asleep on their chairs and being rudely awakened by their landlady stamping her foot, unable to bear the thought of a single line of her reading going unnoticed. Rosa was only too aware that her housemates were fit to drop. She herself was able to make it all the way through only because she'd slept all day, but the others were dreaming of their beds. Keen to keep both sides happy—by giving Jeanne the satisfaction of educating her boarders, all while helping the girls stay awake—Rosa had a stroke of genius that would have made Terese Ost proud. She had to find a way to get the other girls involved in the literary soirées so that each of them would realize how important they were to the group. And so it was with this educational goal in mind that our naïve young socialist took a sip of steaming-hot tea and said:

"I honestly can't wait to hear the rest of the historical novel, but before we begin, I wonder if one of us might by any chance have penned a little something of her own. Any old thing! Perhaps a poem or a short story. It might be nice to hear it, don't you think?"

Quizzical looks. Young Jacqueline, the Haitian who until then seemed to have taken a vow of silence, leapt to her feet.

"I did, I did! I wrote a story!"

"A story?" Heather chipped in, having read Rosa's mind.

"Yes, a story. Would you like to hear it?"

Jeanne brandished her veto. It was put to a vote. The "Ayes" won with 80%. Jacqueline went upstairs and returned with a stack of handwritten papers covered with crossed-out words. She sat back down in her armchair, beaming with pride. Eight surprised eyes demanded to be entertained. The lithe Haitian began to speak.

140

"I wrote this little story for my mother."

Jeanne took off her glasses and snapped her book shut.

"For your mother?" Jeanne asked, incredulously.

"Yes, Jeanne. It's a fifteen-page story."

"I didn't know you wrote. So, what's it about then?"

"It's a little strange. It's... uh... it's called 'The Toad.' I've pitched it to publishers, but they all turned it down. Each of the stories is about an animal. It's a kind of bestiary."

The three boarders exchanged looks of surprise and admiration. A story from Jacqueline, their housemate who never spoke! At last, a window onto the enigmatic soul of the Caribbean beauty. Rosa practically quivered with joy.

"Go on, read! We wanna hear your story," she urged, pressing her hands to her heart.

Perdita nodded enthusiastically and Heather clapped her hands and crowed, "All riiight!"

Jacqueline blushed and lowered her eyes.

"I don't know if you'll like it," she said, shyly.

"Well, go on then with yer Haitian story," Jeanne sighed.

"Oh, well, it... uh, it doesn't have much to do with Haiti. At least, I don't think it does. Perhaps some might detect an allegory for otherness in one of the characters or a voodoo metaphor, but read into it what you will."

"Read, Jacqueline, read!" Rosa shouted.

Loftily, Jacqueline held her manuscript up to her nose, donned a pair of reading glasses that made her look like a governor general, took a deep breath, and began to read, her diction impeccable.

"Krik?" Jacqueline cleared her throat. "Krak!"

The Toad; or the Destiny of a Batrachian

One freezing February morning, after a dreamless night, Madame Bourdeau woke eight minutes earlier than usual. She stared at the red numbers on her alarm clock for a few seconds then turned to peck her husband, Florent, on the cheek.

Jacqueline looked over her glasses to find three captivated faces and six wide eyes. It was her voice more than anything that fascinated the girls. They had little interest in Madame Bourdeau's early mornings, but they drank in each and every phoneme in all its purity, with a focus that would have put to shame Lúcia, Francisco, and Jacinta as they listened to the Virgin Mary at Fátima. They listened to Jacqueline the way you listen to Maria Callas for the first time. Jeanne flicked through the book on her lap, only half listening to Jacqueline's story.

"Go on!" the three young women begged.

She leaned over, her eyes still closed, to kiss Monsieur Bourdeau's cheek. But her lips closed on emptiness, failing to find her husband's cheek. Madame Bourdeau opened her eyes and realized that the place Monsieur Bourdeau had occupied in the marital bed for seventeen years was empty. The covers lay still against the mattress, the pillow visible. Never before had Monsieur

Bourdeau arisen before his wife. Ever. It was an order as immutable as the movements of the moon and the sun. Madame Bourdeau called out to her absent husband in a thin, reedy voice.

"Florent? Florent? Are you there, Florent?" The only answer was a sad croak that came out from beneath the covers, which Madame Bourdeau pulled back with a jerk. There before her eyes, on the immaculate white sheet, a warty, slobbery toad looked up at her with bulging eyes. Madame Bourdeau let out a high-pitched shriek: "Florent!" The visibly frightened toad hopped up and down three times and replied, "Croooak, croooak, croooak."

Jacqueline had to stop reading to let her three young housemates get over their fit of giggles. Heather wiped away a tear. Jeanne drummed her toes against the floor. Pleased at the effect she was having, Jacqueline carried on reading.

"Florent! Oh my God! What a horrible creature! Scram, you ugly thing! What have you done with my husband? I kissed him goodnight and now I've woken up next to a frightful green toad." The batrachian croaked twice more. Standing now beside the bed, Madame Bourdeau buried her face in her hands.

"Where are you, Florent?"

The toad croaked again. Suddenly Madame Bourdeau realized what had happened...

Once again, Jacqueline had to pause as Heather and Rosa clutched their sides, quivering with laughter. Perdita had been reduced to a pile of trembling rags, her brown eyes wet with tears.

"It's amaaazing!" Rosa purred.

"Oh! Oh, my ribs.... Owww!" Perdita wailed.

"Oh, my cheeks! Let me laugh! Please, stop! I can't take any more," Heather rhapsodized.

"Oh come on. It's crap," Jeanne cut in, straight to the point as ever.

The laughter died immediately. Jacqueline's smile turned to astonishment.

"I've never heard anything so stupid. Come on! A woman wakes up one morning to find her husband turned into a toad. I mean, seriously! It's ridiculous. It's not realistic. Talk about a pile of garbage."

Jeanne was clearly worked up by Jacqueline's story.

Rosa rushed to the rescue of the dismayed author.

"No, no, Jeanne! It's an allegory. Jacqueline has written a parable. She's obviously turned the fairy tale on its head—the one where the princess kisses the frog to get him to turn into a prince—to expose the alienation felt by middle-class women. Madame Bourdeau has just realized she's a subjugated wife. This will probably be followed by a phase of emancipation not unlike the realization by the proletariat that the structures are crushing them. She's scared by the image this newfound awareness has created. Sure, Jacqueline is taking a humorous approach to a serious subject, but it's not uncommon. Laughter is often a way to draw the attention of oppressed women. They'll recognize themselves in this story of metamorphosis. In fact, it reminds me of a tale by a certain early-twentieth-century writer in Prague..."

Heather, suddenly caught up in the discussion, decided to bring an English-Canadian perspective to the debate. Putting on her best CBC accent, she intoned:

"Tempting though it may be, I think we must resist any parallels with Kafka's insect. If you ask me, the key to this story lies much closer to home. It's a textbook case of reappropriating an insult with a postmodern twist. The name Bourdeau is clearly French-Canadian—"

"Québécois!" Jeanne thundered.

"Whatever," the blonde from Ontario went on. "You say potayto, I say potahto. Anyone can see that the toad is clearly a reference to the 'French frog' insult used by English speakers to hold francophones up to ridicule. Florent Bourdeau is asserting his frog identity. This is all about reappropriating an insult. You know what I mean?"

"I get it," Rosa went on. "Score one to you, Heather! I hadn't considered it that way. In other words, the Bourdeaus represent an allegory of Canada's two solitudes, right? We should be picturing Madame Bourdeau as an Ontarian or Manitoban who married a Québécois?"

"Not necessarily," Heather replied. It wouldn't surprise me to find out later in the story that Madame Bourdeau is actually an aristocrat who married a pleb, which would support your materialist approach."

Perdita rolled her tired eyes. It was all gibberish to her.

"I have another idea," she cut in. "Maybe Jacqueline has written a short story about food. If you ask me,

Monsieur Bourdeau's legs are going to wind up served in dill sauce in the last paragraph. Wouldn't that be a delicious twist!"

The four women burst into gales of laughter that exhausted the last remaining millilitres of their landlady's patience. Forever after, Heather would weep for Haiti, Rosa would eagerly wait for the peaches to arrive from Ontario every August, and Jacqueline would pray for war-torn Guruistan. Jeanne shot Rosa a blank look, refusing to let her finish her commentary.

"Come on! Our Jacqueline here's just spoutin' nonsense, if you ask me. Don't think for a minute folks round here are gonna see themselves in her story... For starters, we don't even know where or when it takes place. And anyway, it ain't stories about husbands being turned into toads that are gonna set women free! No way is some Czech guy who's been dead and buried for years gonna tell the women of Quebec how to liberate themselves."

There was an awkward silence. A fly buzzed. The girls stared at the floor. Jacqueline set down her story and went back to the silent world she wished she'd never left. She hadn't had any intention of "coming to a realization." She'd just picked up a pen to write down a funny story she'd dreamt up. Jeanne was right. She was off her head. Jacqueline stood up, walked slowly over to the hearth where a few embers still glowed, and threw her manuscript into the fire. It went up in flames at once. The batrachian's fate would never be known. Jacqueline sat back down on her wooden chair.

Jeanne stared at the flames for a moment, swallowed, clicked her tongue, put her reading glasses back on, and, in a solemn voice and an accent the girls had never heard her use before, announced the reading she had chosen for their literary soirée.

"This evening, you will have the pleasure of hearing a passage from the latest historical novel by Michou Minou—a woman born in Quebec, by the way—entitled *Madame Autrefois*, which recounts the real-life story of our country's first *francophone* surgeon. You will be astonished by her ability to recreate the atmosphere of the nineteenth century, right down to the tiniest detail. Not a single facet of life from the time has escaped the notice of this master of realism. The passage I've chosen to read for you is one in which Madame Autrefois walks in on her husband as he is writing a poem to his lover, Lady Pepperpot."

Rosa raised her eyes heavenward. Jeanne began reading in a schoolmistress voice, stressing every letter and pretending to be overcome by the passages where Dr. Autrefois subjects his poor sobbing wife to some humiliation or other, or slowing to dwell on the nostalgia the poor French colonist feels for her homeland.

Chapter CCLXXVIII

Exhausted by a long day spent contemplating the ice floes drifting along the St. Lawrence River, a river seemingly made for giants, Madame Autrefois wearily waved away her servant Marie-Louise, a pleasant red-headed girl of good country stock from the county of

Nicolet, who, like every other evening, was wearing a coarse, greenish-yellow cloth dress imported from the United States and a white cotton scarf knotted beneath her chin, which only served to contrast, even more violently, the rosiness of her broad peasant cheeks, the cheeks of peasant women who had cleared the immense land of theirs, a windswept land where Dr. Autrefois, a Conservative as blue as any hanged man, had, in a fit of Christian philanthropy, dragged poor Amélie Autrefois, née Dearie, despite her being a lass of delicate constitution who had almost been carried off by consumption no fewer than four times already, and who, that evening, returned to her novel by Madame Oareyre, the great literary talent of Île-de-France whom History was to consign to oblivion. Madame Autrefois would sigh at each description of the intoxicating gatherings of the young, nubile heroines in those novels that reminded her of the excesses of Paris and the folles nuits at Versailles. The cold December wind rattled the roof of the fine home on Rue Saint-Paul, its rafters made from the pure, hard maple trees that grew on the land, a conquered land that she dreamt of abandoning daily, eager to return to her beloved France where her ancestors lay in peace. Yet again that very day, she had had the unpleasant experience of overhearing two gentlemen speaking in English in her town in Lower Canada, once New France, a town that was losing a little more of its French identity by the day. Madame Autrefois turned a page of the book now yellowed by the long and perilous transatlantic crossing, then decided otherwise and began to re-read the page she had just finished. Then began a long sigh that was, ultimately, not as long as she had at first feared. In a haughty motion that was entirely befitting of her rank, she stroked the white lace on the sleeve of her immaculate nightgown. She sighed a second time. This time the sigh was rather lengthy, although not as long as the terrible squall that was now threatening to carry off the roof. Madame Autrefois sighed a third time, a long French sigh that reminded her of the virile French sighs of her father, Pierre Dearie, whose great-grandfather had been a notary in Rollinzehay-sur-Isère before the war. Her sigh was interrupted by the thin voice of Marie-Louise.

"Would madame like some tea?"

Tea! Tea! Why in God's name were people around here so fond of all things English? Wasn't it enough they had been conquered? Were they now to scald themselves with cups of piping-hot humiliation served with a splash of milk?

"No, Marie-Louise. I do not want your tea!"

Rosa had heard of the story before. She mused that, had she been looking for the wind in Montreal back in that day and age, it wouldn't have taken her very long at all, given the weather system that was swirling around the neurasthenic Madame Autrefois. Dr. Autrefois, who had founded the first French-language hospital in Montreal, had apparently been romantically involved with the wife of his rival, Dr. Pepperpot, a pink-faced Englishman rendered impotent after a particularly nasty bout of plum pudding indigestion. Michou Minou, the celebrated author of a series of popular historical novels, had written an eight-hundred-page opus about him, which the entire province had been lapping up for weeks. The novel was so successful, and the writing so convincing, that more than a few women had been seen berating the bust of the late Dr. Autrefois that stood in the middle of the lobby of the Hôpital du Précieux Sang. The Société Saint-Jean-Baptiste went so far as to award the novel its literary prize. Rosa, you will understand, had no time whatsoever for tales of the petty problems of the middle class, be it in French Canada, Hungary, America, or Papua New Guinea. A look of solemn intensity came over the other guests. As their landlady caught her breath before launching into a new page, a question welled up inside Rosa and slipped out like a belch. Once again, that strange hook tugged upwards on the right side of her upper lip.

"What does Madame Autrefois have to do with us?"

Jeanne was dumbfounded.

"What kind of question is that! It's a story about our collective memory! We must remember! That man humiliated his wife. We have a duty to her to remember!"

"A duty to remember?" Rosa repeated.

"Yes. It's our duty to remember her."

"Does remembering her really have to take up eight hundred pages of our precious lives? Eight hundred trees from our forests?"

"Excuse me, young lady, this is a bestseller we're talkin' about here! Every description is amazingly true to life. This book is the result of years of research into Madame Autrefois' personal archives. There's even a detailed description of all her hats in Chapter CCCVII."

"Unless you happen to be a hatmaker, I'm afraid I just don't see the point."

Jeanne smacked the book shut. The other girls stared hard at the bottom of their teacups. All could foresee a door slamming shut in the very near future.

"But you of all people should know, Little Miss Know-It-All, that what is realistic is beautiful."

"Maybe, but not everything that's realistic is necessarily real. If I told you, for example, that I had tea with Fidel Castro and Jimmy Carter on October 3 of last year, that sounds realistic enough, but that doesn't mean it's true."

"But we're talking about a great writer! She's won awards!"

"Fair enough, Jeanne," said Rosa. "Let's suppose this is a work of the highest quality. What good is it to us today? Am I going to change the way I live because Dr. Autrefois was rolling around in the hay with his rival's wife in 1845?"

"No, but you should realize that his slight left its mark on all women. Poor Madame Autrefois' story can serve as a lesson, and help you avoid her sad fate."

"I don't see what's so sad about belonging to the middle class in nineteenth-century Montreal, back when everyone else was dying from cold, hunger, and epidemics. I meant what I said: Not everything realistic is necessarily real. And not everything real is necessarily useful to anyone." (This last word grated in particular on poor Rosa's palate. She still had no idea that she may as well have been talking to the wall.) "If I tell you, for example, that on March 16, 1992, at 7:12 p.m., Aunt Zenaida cleaned her oven, that's all true enough and verifiable, but it doesn't help any of us live our lives today. In fact, we could all care less..."

Jeanne leapt to her feet, cutting her off. She stomped out of the parlour, slamming the door behind her.

"If that's how you feel about it, you'll just have to do without the rest of Madame Autrefois' story!"

The tension in the room had grabbed all the other women by the throat. None of them seemed able to find a way to defuse the situation. Perdita tried to open her mouth, but it was as if she was petrified with fear. The four housemates found themselves alone with their tea. They heard their landlady slam the door to her room. They knew they still had fifteen minutes before curfew. Each wanted to give Rosa a piece of her mind, to explain that her literary outpouring had only stoked Jeanne's ire, that they'd likely all be eating nothing but turnip soup for a week. And yet the incident had ignited in them a flame of revolt they'd all but forgotten. Somewhere between delight at no longer being subjected to a reading from *Madame Autrefois* and fear at what Jeanne Joyal's vengeance might look like, a feeling resembling gratitude reared its victorious little head and smiled at Rosa. Something not unlike the first crack in the Berlin Wall, the first Black woman to sit at the front of the bus, the first retreat of the German army before Stalingrad. Shaken and a little ashamed at once again having proved herself incapable of being able to tell the difference between when it is important to speak up and when she should simply keep quiet, Rosa spent the minutes that remained before curfew trying to draw a smile from her housemates with her account of the previous night at the Butler Motor Hotel, before hopping back on the southbound number 55 bus. The kerfuffle at the reading circle had left her exhausted, and she fell asleep as the bus turned onto Saint-Urbain, dreaming of serving tea to a bunch of people dressed in Italian suits as they sat around a table. As she drew closer with her teapot, she recognized Pierre Elliott Trudeau, Madame Autrefois, Sri Satyanarayana, and several other very old people she didn't know. They invited her to sit with them. Rosa let out a long and resounding "No," which jolted her awake. The bus driver eyed her in amusement.

Gillian was waiting for her in the lobby when she got to the hotel, and they sat down for a chat in the little office. Gillian was wearing a strange outfit: a leather bra with cups in the shape of maple leaves and very short jean shorts with the word CANADA emblazoned in huge fluorescent letters across her bum. It had been a gift from the owner of the Butler Motor Hotel, a cabinet minister and staunch federalist, she explained. She'd refused to wear the outfit at first, on purely aesthetic grounds (orange really wasn't her colour), but the bespectacled gentleman had won her over with the promise of five hundred dollars every night she walked the streets in it. The sly old devil had also promised her a bonus if she got some of the other girls to wear the same uniform, but all that was strictly between the two of them, she told Rosa. The minister had insisted they keep the whole thing under wraps. Gillian would often write for a few minutes before heading back out. She explained to Rosa that she was putting the finishing touches to a piece of autofiction that explored her sense of alienation from her own body. At the word "alienation," Rosa demanded Gillian read from her novel there and then. The redhead hesitated at first, then finally relented. The novel was entitled *Clitoris*. It was a working title, of course; it could always be tweaked later if a publisher agreed to take it on.

"Will you read me a bit?"

"You're such a sweetheart!"

Gillian struck a provocative pose, tugged an already plunging neckline down until it left nothing to the imagination, and began to read in a suave voice.

Clitoris

It's this clitoris as I see it, or rather as I saw it, because I will never see again. This clitoris, jewel and pustule of every woman, this clitoris that glistens for and by itself. Pink dot in the black of night. Pink night in the black of my fists. Accursed veins...

And so it went on. Rosa applauded when Gillian got to the end.

"It's wonderful, Gillian. Incredibly beautiful. You absolutely have to try to find a publisher for it. I'm sure it'll be a huge success."

"It's not the first time someone's told me that. I've already sent it to a few places, even in France. I'm waiting to hear back."

An answer wasn't long in coming. In January 2001, a prestigious French publisher agreed to publish Gillian's manuscript, without changing a thing. She was given the red-carpet treatment all across Europe and welcomed with open arms. *Clitoris* became an overnight success the world over. The *Étoile de Montréal* even devoted half of its Arts & Entertainment supplement to it. On more than one occasion. One reviewer could barely contain himself: "This novel edifies even the paper and the ink that went into its creation, underscoring the author's intelligence and uncommonly powerful writing. The descriptions of the hell the narrator experienced, although occasionally crude, are incredibly necessary. Let's be clear: *Clitoris* is the strongest possible denunciation of the pitiful excuses that are used to exploit the female body. In all honesty, this heartbreaking cry for help transcends its art." In the weeks after it was published, the novel was translated into thirty-four different languages, including Catalan and Hindi. Banned in Sweden and the United States, it was in Europe's German-speaking countries that the novel proved most popular, flying off library and bookstore shelves from Vienna to Rügen. Special programs were devoted to it on all the German channels. A week after the German edition came out, *Der Spiegel* accompanied its feature article entitled *Klitoris: das kanadische Skandalbuch* with a provocative bust shot of Gillian touching the index finger of her right hand to her tongue. The red-hot literary sensation led to all kinds of problems in locales that were unused to such works. On the train from Vöcklabruck to Salzburg, for example, young

Maximilian Brandstätter, a student in his final year of secondary school in Neumarkt am Wallersee, brazenly indulged in a bit of self-gratification in an empty compartment of the train he was riding home after his final Tuesday class. While Max, a well-mannered boy who had been brought up in a prim and proper Austrian household, did not make a habit of such behaviour, he had been unable to contain himself upon opening Gillian's novel (carefully concealed in his Latin textbook), alas, at the very moment the ticket inspector of the Austrian Federal Railways flung open the compartment door with a perfunctory "Fahrkarten, bitte!" Young Max was arrested and hauled off to the Salzburg police station, where his mother (an upstanding woman from Steiermark who had raised her son in the staunchest Catholic tradition), crimson with shame, went to pick up the teenage boy, who stood accused of gross indecency, molesting a federal railway employee, and vandalism for having soiled the royal blue compartment seats, which had to be scrubbed clean with the most caustic of chemicals and the toughest of brushes. Germany had already lost count of the innumerable incidents and household spats set off by the book, not to mention the futile howls of rage from archbishops the length and breadth of Central Europe. It was decided at an extraordinary sitting of the Bundestag that distribution of the accursed novel would be prohibited, which only octupled sales. Gillian became a rich woman. She was able to go back to New York, where she bought a spectacular loft in Lower Manhattan overlooking the East River. True to her eccentric ways, she organized, every Tuesday morning, a literary breakfast she hosted in Manhattan's highest restaurant—a tribute to the two white phalluses that stood proudly at the tip of her island. On September 11, 2001, Allah answered Frau Brandstätter's prayers and divine retribution struck down Gillian, who went off to join the ranks of literary martyrs.

::

Sometime during the fourth week of November 2000, Montreal treated Rosa to another revelation. One chilly, orange-tinged morning, Constable Savoie turned up in plain clothes in the Butler lobby. The sinister-looking Indian man who took over from Rosa every morning knocked nervously on the door of the ladies' washroom, where Rosa was powdering her nose while she waited for her admirer. "The Big Red Acadian's here. Miss Rosa, the Big Red Acadian's here," he said, loud enough for Savoie to hear him. Rosa finished doing her hair and went out to meet her suitor. He seemed more dashing than ever that particular morning, dressed in a pair of pants that showed off his divine posterior and a tight-fitting shirt that revealed, beneath its thin layer of white cloth, a Schwarzeneggerian set of muscles. Ever the perfect gentleman, as all Acadian men are, he pecked young Rosa on the cheek, her complexion taking three seconds to turn the same colour as her companion's hair. For nearly three weeks now, Savoie had been picking Rosa up every morning and taking her for a cappuccino on the corner of Saint-Urbain and Sainte-Catherine before walking her to the bus stop. His patient courting gradually wore away the pride of the young Gaspé girl, as surely and slowly as the waters of the Gulf of St. Lawrence had bored the hole in Percé Rock. No one was in any rush. Rosa once asked him whether the respect he showed her was down to the age difference between them or to some religious custom or other. Savoie considered the matter for a long time, then murmured in her ear, in the accent that made her ovulate: "It's not wot you have dat makes a body proud, it's knowin' dat you'll have it." It hadn't taken long for him to figure out the effect his accent had on our little Rosa, and he sprinkled his local expressions into their conversations the way some men douse themselves in cologne. Despite being born and bred in the path of the strong winds of Kouchibouguac National Park, and although he was as much a depository for his culture as any Leblanc or Arseneault, he had been in Montreal for twenty years and, while there was no denying his Maritime roots, nor could he be neatly filed away alongside one of those degrading multicultural dolls on the Canadian Heritage brochures. Whenever young Rosa was around, he laid it on nice and thick. Given the chance, he'd have turned up at the Butler accompanied by a fiddle or an accordion. As for Rosa, her naiveté in matters of seduction could be traced back to a youth that had been devoted to the world of ideas and entirely lacking in affairs of the heart. When it came to anything other than dialectics, history, or literature, it wasn't hard to pull the wool over our little Rosa's eyes. Holding Savoie's hand as they strolled along Boulevard Saint-Laurent, Rosa no longer felt the slightest need to sing to herself or fret about Guatemalan sweat-shops. Sometimes when she was in the company of that particular descendant of a deported Acadian, she would even forget about the wind.

On that brisk November morning, Rosa and Savoie were walking back up Boulevard Saint-Laurent. They didn't stop off at Café République for their morning coffee. On that particular day, Savoie had a surprise for his sweetheart. When they reached the corner of Sherbrooke and Saint-Laurent, Rosa realized that the boulevard had been closed off to traffic and that two rows of Montrealers of every possible colour lined each side of the street, speaking every possible language. The atmosphere was part village fair, part breathless anticipation. By all appearances, some had been waiting on their folding chairs since dawn. Women came out of Café Dépôt carrying steaming cups of coffee.

"What in the world is going on?"

It was like the coronation of Her Majesty Queen Elizabeth II. Rosa kept expecting a gilt-covered horse-drawn carriage to appear at any moment, bearing some capitalist princess with perfect teeth. Savoie grinned.

"It's the Return of the Snow Geese!"

As though to prove what he'd just said, a huge snow goose mascot handed Rosa a flyer. The mass of feathers with the human inside continued making its way south.

The Return of the Snow Geese

The snow goose (Anser caerulescens) *nests around Baffin Bay. Every fall, millions of geese leave the Far North for the centre of the United States, where they spend the winter. For as far back as anyone can remember, the graceful birds have stopped at Cap-Tourmente, Baie-du-Febvre, and Montmagny, a little further to the east along the St. Lawrence Valley. This year, birders across the Far North have noted that the absence of the westerly wind—a situation that has affected all of northeastern North America since August—has changed the species' migratory habits. Given the lack of wind from the west, the flight corridor for millions of birds has shifted westward, and migration has been delayed by a month. Thanks to a clever triangulation method employed by international wind expert Dr. Peder Pedersen, co-director of the Royal Institute for Wind Energy Research in Copenhagen; Professor Ingeborg Borgman, his German counterpart from Stralsund University; and their cook and personal interpreter who follows them on their travels and insists on remaining anonymous, GLUM has learned that a colony of snow geese is headed straight for Montreal and should reach the city on November 22 at 8:22 a.m. on the dot. The calculations by the team of European researchers are precise enough to predict that Boulevard Saint-Laurent will align with the flight path of the geese who, this year, for reasons that remain a mystery, are flying barely two metres above the ground. The boulevard will therefore be closed for the day so as not to interfere with the geese's southerly migration. Montrealers are invited to admire this rare phenomenon from either side of the street, and are reminded to show respect for the birds. We ask that members of the public allow the birds to progress unimpeded towards their final destination since the annual migration has already been delayed by more than three weeks due to global warming in Quebec's Far North. Spectators are urged to avoid feeding the birds and to remain silent while the geese are in flight. GLUM, in collaboration with the City of Montreal, is proud to invite you to the very first Return of the Snow Geese.*

Rosa couldn't believe it. Not only had the lack of wind transformed her village into a place where old people saw out their final days, it had also knocked the migrating snow geese off course. On either side of Boulevard Saint-Laurent, people were counting down the minutes until the birds arrived. Two other human geese, smaller this time, were waddling through the crowd, handing people a pen and a piece of paper. Some grabbed the pen and signed a document that Rosa couldn't make out, while others laughed and turned away. The couple dressed up as geese walked up to Rosa and Réjean. They were Bob and Tina, they said. From Victoria. They were sure they'd seen Rosa somewhere before.

"Aren't you that girl who cried at Trudeau's funeral? You poor thing. Are you better now? We cried too."

Rosa swore she had no idea what they were talking about, that they must be mixing her up with someone

161

else, that there'd been some mistake. The couple from Victoria were trying to get the crowd to sign a petition that, in their words, was "very important for all Canadians." Rosa took a closer look.

We, the undersigned, urge the Government of Canada to formally submit a request to the Vatican authorities to immediately beatify the late Pierre Elliott Trudeau. This would be a worthy tribute to the greatest man to ever walk on Canadian soil. We worship and accept him as our personal, spiritual saviour.

Savoie signed without giving it a second thought, but Rosa was pensive. Worship the man? Would her mother have approved? She knew that the whole country was still mourning the illustrious prime minister, but something inside her prevented her from signing the document. She couldn't have said exactly why. That's just how it was.

"I'll have to... I'll have to give it some thought," she said.

The human goose snatched back the pen. Pursing her lips, she asked if Rosa was "a separatist." Rosa didn't know what to reply. She whispered that she was looking for the wind. The couple turned and walked away, looking back one last time to glare at her. The geese disappeared into the crowd, wiggling their big feather derrières as they waddled left and right. She had never seen anything more ridiculous in all her life, Rosa thought to herself.

Savoie took Rosa's hand when they reached the corner of Prince-Arthur and Saint-Laurent. Suddenly, from a northerly direction, they heard a sound they were unused to hearing in the city. An infinitely sad and listless *hoonk, hoonk, hoonk*. The snow geese were there. The birds were flying a metre and a half above the ground at fifty kilometres an hour. The boulevard had been reduced to one long goose honk. A honk that had begun on Baffin Island and would end in West Virginia. The people of Montreal were fascinated. Rapt. No one thought to speak. People reached out to grab a hand, any hand. Serbs held hands with Croats, an obese millionaire took a filthy, scrawny vagrant by the hand. A crowd that stretched all along the boulevard, right up to Highway 40, stood and watched for two hours as half a million geese flew through the city on their way to summer. Everyone ignored the store displays, written in every single one of the world's languages. Life was nothing but one long, white, feathery line, honking its way south, even though the boulevard is, as everyone knows, a one-way street headed north. Rosa felt a breeze against her skin; it was the draft generated as the geese beat their huge wings. The filthy pavement became gradually covered in a white carpet of down left behind by the birds' mesmerizing flight. The feathers landed in women's hair and got caught up in the mustaches of tearful Portuguese men who, for those two whole hours, had completely forgotten they would never see their beloved Azores again. An Irishwoman forgot the wrongs done to the children of her island and folded her palms over her redhead heart. A Jewish woman's thoughts turned to Christ on the cross, a priest flung his clerical collar to the ground, sobbing, "Treblinka..." The last of the geese continued on its leisurely flight before the hypnotized crowd. Everyone had stopped breathing. Stopped believing. Stopped sneering. They just were.

Jolted as if by an electric current, Rosa let go of Savoie's hand and ran out into the middle of the feather-covered street. She ran, slipped, fell, picked herself up, ran some more, fell a second time, and scraped her right knee, which began to bleed, leaving a red trail behind her along the immaculate boulevard. She limped her way to the Ex-Centris cinema, her breathing ragged. Rosa fell a third time. Two huge hands, powered by an unknown force, scooped her up by the waist. With incredible strength, Savoie set her down on his shoulders, striding forward to help her catch up to the snow geese. The blood continued to trickle down Rosa's leg and onto the tip of her shoe before dropping onto the carpet of white. It was as if the towering red-haired man was melting, leaving splotches of his being in his wake. The rider and her mount were gasping as they reached the corner of Sherbrooke and Saint-Laurent, where Saint-Laurent abruptly dips down towards the city centre, and from where a wonderful view can be had on any bright and clear morning such as that one, a view that included the St. Lawrence River Valley and, if you were to squint a little, perhaps even all the way to the United States. Savoie and Rosa gazed at the geese that hadn't followed the dip in the street, some heading southeast, some southwest, in a clattering, ascending migration. The geese had split into two equal groups, two huge V-shaped formations that were headed for more clement skies, obeying an instinct that would lead them to the place they could finally rest. Rosa shouted as she pointed at the two groups, striking a positively papal pose for a fraction of a second. By the time Rosa and Savoie made their way back, the crowd who had come to see the Return of the Snow Geese had cleared the street of its feathers—a memento by which to remember those two epiphanic hours—and scattered east and west, back to their homes. The two sweethearts were in a daze, as though they had dreamt the whole thing. All that remained before them was a long ribbon of pavement, stretching to the north. Rosa stopped by a drugstore for a bandage to put on her still-bleeding knee. Savoie insisted on taking her home. It was almost noon, after all, and she hadn't eaten or slept since the day before.

In the back seat of the cab that took them to Villeray, they closed their eyes, imagining themselves for the length of a taxi ride to be two snow geese who'd been flying south side by side, only to be separated by fate upon reaching Sherbrooke. Rosa figured the geese were all heading to the same spot and would reunite in some American cotton field. Savoie was fairly sure that the pair of geese would probably never see each other again, that entire avian families had been separated by the migration, and he could hardly bear the thought. He drew Rosa in closer, slowly, and she let him. She rested her head on his shoulder and, for the first time, smelled his musky redhead smell. It was a smell she was sure she knew from somewhere; it wasn't new to her. For once, Rosa wanted to say something, but she didn't know how. She wanted to know what the future would be like, because Réjean never mentioned the future. Did he see a future for them? Running through the list of everyone she knew, she realized she'd never learned to open up to anyone about her "feelings." In fact, she often wondered if she even had any to speak of. Her ignorance was tinged with the fear she might scare away Réjean with her seriousness. Truth be told, our little Rosa had spent many an hour picturing a future with Réjean, had even chosen names for their children, and had already decided they would spend their Saturday evenings drinking camomile tea and listening to Mozart. Mozart or Bach, she hadn't made her mind up yet. She'd have to think about it some more. If she closed her eyes, the words would come more easily, she thought to herself, and she'd be able to get Réjean to decide between the Austrian and the German.

"Réjean..."

"Yes."

"Do you... do you know much about birds?"

"Why?"

"Do you think those geese would be able to fly all the way to Cuba?"

"To Cuba? No. I think they only go as far as the United States, to Virginia or Maryland."

"Do you... do you think the geese we just saw form couples?"

"Of course they do! How do you think they reproduce?"

"I just mean, do you think they stay together long?"

"I don't know, Rosa. Why are you asking?"

"Well, I was wondering how they tell each other apart. They all look alike to me."

"I think it's by the sound they make. Each goose makes its own sound. It all sounds the same to us, but they can tell the difference. It's like when I heard your accent for the first time. It's as though I'd recognized you from among a thousand other geese."

Rosa swallowed. No one had ever said anything like that to her before. She pressed on:

"And if you heard another goose that had my accent, would you go after her?"

"No way. It's not just the accent, Rosa. It's... I don't know. It's something you just feel."

"Feel where?"

"I can't explain it. It's like our two voices sound alike, like one is exactly like the other, only an octave higher. It's like when I call my sister in Moncton. She talks just like my pops, only an octave higher."

"And my voice. Is that something you'd want to hear for a very long time?"

"Oh, well, I... think... I don't know. I..."

Réjean didn't have time to finish his answer. The taxi was pulling up outside Jeanne's house. When Rosa opened her eyes again, the taxi door was open and Jeanne Joyal was standing on the sidewalk, hands on hips.

"You're late! I was worried!"

Jeanne looked the giant redhead up and down, staring hard at him for a solid minute, until he began to feel uncomfortable, then gave him a manly handshake.

"Jeanne Joyal."

"Réjean Savoie."

Even though the church bells at Saint-Alphonse d'Youville could be heard striking noon, the temperature on Rue du Saint-Ciboire suddenly dropped by four degrees. Savoie tried to reassure the landlady as to his intentions.

"I'm a police officer with the City."

"Uh-huh."

"I brought Rosa home after the Return of the Snow Geese because she hurt her knee."

"She couldn't have taken a taxi by herself?"

Rosa wanted to say something, but she was paralyzed with exhaustion. Making a poor attempt at an Acadian accent, Jeanne Joyal barked:

"Well, *tank* you very much, *mon cher mansieur*, but it's time for Rosa to go to bed now."

Stunned, Réjean didn't know how to respond to the ridicule being heaped upon him by this extraordinary Amazon. For Rosa's sake, he took a step back and began walking to the metro station. The two women continued their awkward conversation once they were back indoors.

"So you're cavorting with men now?"

"Réjean's just a friend. I—"

"Don't gimme that! He's an Acadian. Plus, he's at least forty-three!"

"Well, yes, but have you seen the shape he's in? He can scoop me up by the waist and set me on his shoulders, like I was his little girl."

"Look, Rosa. If you start bringin' men back here, you can find someplace else to live. You know the rules."

"I'm telling you, Jeanne, there's nothing going on between me and Réjean. Our relationship is strictly platonic. I think he might be courting me, but he's discreet and loyal and—"

Jeanne dropped to her knees onto the rug in the hallway.

"Oh thank God! You swear nothing's happened? You're absolutely sure?"

"Honestly. I met him a few weeks ago. He takes me for coffee when I finish my shift in the morning and that's it. He tells me about being a police officer... Jeanne? You're crying, Jeanne."

"I want you to stop seeing that guy. It's terrible! You don't know what you're gettin' yourself into. You're here to find the wind. Not to be flirtin' with Montreal cops."

Jeanne fell into her lodger's arms. Rosa wasn't sure how to react to this unexpected outpouring of emotion. What did it matter to Jeanne who she went out with? Jeanne hurried to her room and locked the door behind her. Rosa went up to her room and fell into a troubled sleep that was punctuated by strange dreams: she and Savoie were snow geese, flying south side by side along Boulevard Saint-Laurent as a captivated crowd looked on. When they got to Sherbrooke, she sensed that her course was steering her away from Savoie and she could hear only his distressed honks. "Wait for me in Maryland!" All she could see was the horse she was riding. It was one of those strange dreams where everything suddenly changes. Now she was following Jeanne, who was wearing a suit of armour and carrying a pennant with three white lilies on it. Their horses were galloping towards an unknown city. The sound of the hoofs from Rosa's horse blended into the clatter of footsteps as Heather, Perdita, and Jacqueline climbed the wooden staircase.

It was time for supper.

CHAPTER 5

Je me souviens

THE KNIVES AND FORKS clinked against the fleur-de-lys plates. Jeanne had decided to let the girls eat alone that Wednesday evening while she prepared a surprise for them. The four housemates weren't used to the luxury of a meal without their landlady and basked in the tranquil silence of the dining room. Jeanne was hard at work in the parlour. They could hear her smart little footsteps on the wooden floor. "These noodles are overcooked," Heather sighed. "In Ontario, we would never have let them get mushy like this in the saucepan." Perdita rose to the bait.

"Not where I'm from either, but what do you expect? This country's not exactly foodie heaven."

Rosa jumped to the defence of her cultural heritage.

"We're not the ones with a winter cabbage festival."

Heather and Perdita pretended not to have heard.

"I'm heading back to Ontario, I swear, just as soon as my French course is over."

"At least you can go home. I have to stay here."

"You're welcome to come to Toronto, you know. It's a very welcoming city. There are plenty of immigrants from Guruistan who live there, and they seem perfectly happy. You're not seriously going to stay here, are you?"

"I don't know, Heather."

"I've got nothing against the place, but it's hard to feel at home here. Quebecers are a little set in their ways..."

Rosa couldn't believe her ears. She opened her eyes wide, as though to listen harder to the conversation.

Heather noticed her expression and tried to walk back some of what she'd just said.

"But you're different, Rosa. You're not like the others."

"Yeah," said Perdita. "You're not the same. And anyway, you're from the Gaspé, right?"

What can you say when a bucket full of seaweed has just been flung in your face?

"But the Gaspé is part of Quebec, you know. I'm both a Quebecer and a Gaspesian. Maybe you're both just homesick. Things aren't so bad here."

Heather lowered her eyes.

"Look, Rosa. We don't mean to insult you, but sometimes, you know, your fellow Quebecers can be a little... how should I put this? Let's just say they're not so fond of foreigners. You can see it, you can feel it."

"I think the word you're looking for is 'xenophobic,'" Perdita said.

"That's it! They're xenophobic!"

Rosa was upset.

"Oh really? And just how do you measure xenophobia?"

Heather bit her tongue.

"Well, that's what everyone says."

"Well, I'm not everyone and neither are you. As far as I can tell, you're all here working or studying and I'm the one who doesn't have a cent to my name."

"That has nothing to do with it. You can be a millionaire and still be ostracized."

"I should be so lucky!" chuckled Jacqueline, trying to calm the gathering storm.

Rosa sighed.

"Fine. I just hope one day you all find yourselves in a country where you'll be welcomed with open arms: somewhere like Japan, Germany, or Russia. You can send me a postcard. Let me know if a day goes past without your roots being thrown in your face. You're complaining with a full belly, if you ask me."

"If only it wasn't full of these awful noodles," Perdita deadpanned.

Jacqueline and Rosa then sat in stunned silence as they were treated to a litany of complaints against the people of New France.

"They drive like lunatics!"

"They don't look out for pedestrians!"

"They don't learn a thing at school!"

"They can barely speak their own language, and want to impose it on everyone else!"

"They're fat!"

"They're lazy!"

"The women are fishwives!"

"The men are wimps!"

"Their hospitals are falling apart!"

"They have no class!"

"They have no sense of humour!"

"Hockey and fries are all they understand!"

"They live off immigrants' backs!"

"They never stop whining!"

At the very moment the accusations were flying around Jeanne Joyal's dining room, thousands of kilometres away, three American students sitting in a bar in Berlin had just reached exactly the same conclusions about the Germans, although they said "soccer," not "hockey." In Toronto, two Brazilian girls were pointing fingers at the people of Upper Canada, although they left out the word "fries." In fact, if you listened carefully, all around the world a chorus of complaints could be heard, with everyone blaming everyone else. Jacqueline looked from left to right and back. The bombardment over, a soothing silence returned to the room. The Haitian girl, visibly irritated, looked the others square in the eye.

"You're absolutely right. They should all be sent to the gas chamber or sold as slaves."

With that, she stood up and walked out of the room.

Rosa was thunderstruck. In the great cast of humanity, she had always thought of herself first and foremost as Rosa Ost, daughter of Terese Ost, the unionist and socialist. Although she had always accepted she was a product of where she came from, she had never thought of herself as anything other than upstanding and virtuous. She didn't drive, didn't impose anything on anyone, was of normal weight, worked like crazy, and didn't understand the first thing about either hockey or fries. Most importantly of all, she had come to see in Perdita and Heather the kindness of the sisters that fate had denied her. The salvo of angry grievances fired her way had knocked the wind out of her. After all, it had been her, and no one else, the day a family of lost Chinese tourists had wound up in her village, who had managed, with much hand waving and gesturing, to welcome them and show them the blue hues of the Gulf of St. Lawrence. And it was on her shoulder that Heather's head had rested when, not having heard back from the Toronto university she desperately wanted to get into, she'd cried her heart out for two days straight. Rosa was saddened by the Wednesday evening vitriol. As far as she was concerned, Jacqueline, Heather, and Perdita were windows onto a world she would never otherwise have access to, and so she'd always imagined she might be a window onto a little corner of the world for them, too. And yet she'd just been lynched, without fair trial and on trumped-up charges. Sure, Jeanne could be accused of lacking tact and being a bit of a drain on her boarders' social batteries, but it was her home, all the same. It was up to her to set the rules. And if that meant eating roast pork with steamed turnip every Saturday, then so be it! You don't look a gift horse in the mouth! Jeanne could be accused of all the sins in the world, but laziness wasn't one of them. Wasn't it Heather who, just the other week, had refused to make her bed, despite Jeanne blowing a fuse? It was Jacqueline who'd made it in the end, just to calm the hysterics and restore a little peace and quiet to the house.

The dishes were washed, dried, and put away in stony silence. Dark thoughts clouded the expressions that just the day before had been full of girlish camaraderie. A barely repressed desire to lash out at the other girls got in the way of delicately removing every last drop of moisture from each dish. They battered the fragile plates. They fantasized about how certain knives might be used. They dreamt of forks being implanted in foreheads. Rosa was carefully wiping down a glass bowl when it slipped out of her hands and cracked in two on the floor. Jeanne's footsteps could be heard approaching the kitchen. Perdita could *hear* the sweat coming off Rosa. Then, inexplicably, Heather and Perdita bent down, scooped up the pieces of the broken bowl, and hid them up their skirts and between their thighs, the best hiding place they could find in the second and a half they had to get rid of all traces of the accident. The sharp edges of the broken glass ensured the operation was not without risk.

"What's all that racket?" their landlady barked.

"Nothing, nothing at all. It was something in the back alley. A cat..." Perdita replied.

"Darn cats! Did yiz finish the dishes?"

"All put away, Jeanne," Heather purred.

"Yiz're good girls. Right, I'm gonna get Jacqueline. She's upstairs at her desk, writin' more nonsense. I'll wait for y'all in the parlour. Time for a surprise!"

Rosa didn't know what to say. And nothing was said. Sometimes what we say doesn't matter much in the grand scheme of things. Whoever said "Actions speak louder than words" really knew what they were talking about.

The surprise was a big one. Jeanne had prepared a lesson in Quebec history, arranging the chairs in rows so the parlour looked like a classroom, and pinning a detailed map of New France to the wall. She'd also captured their attention by dressing up like a settler from 1670. For once, Jeanne and her boarders were laughing with each other, not at each other. She explained, at great length, how the French colonized the land, complete with a host of details that didn't fail to impress the girls. So vivid and accurate were her descriptions, the girls felt they were actually there. The lesson went on for an hour and a half. To make her presentation even more true to life, Jeanne would occasionally seize a weapon, recreating the heroics of Madeleine de Verchères, miming the Iroquois attacks, scanning the St. Lawrence for any sign of the dastardly English, felling trees, clearing land—in other words, treating the girls to a lively overview of life in the colony. The girls lapped it up. At last, a fun night at Jeanne's. Their landlady couldn't stop smiling.

"I'd noticed a certain lack of interest in Quebec history. I just wanted to be sure my message would get through this time. It's important stuff, if ya ask me. It's my passion. You, Perdita, you're into math. You, Jacqueline, you like writing stories about toads. And you, Rosa, you're chasing after the wind. Then there's Heather, who's learning French. Well, for me, it's all about history."

Rosa was thrilled. After the unpleasantness of supper-time, this was a revelation! Sure, Jeanne was demanding, overbearing, perhaps even a little intransigent. But there was plenty to learn from her. The other girls seemed to have enjoyed the talk as well. Jeanne handed out a sheet with a summary of the lesson she'd just given. The document was entitled "Je me souviens" and listed the key historical events. The girls quickly familiarized themselves with the following prayer.

O people of this land, tabernacle of all the graces and receptacle of Truth, remember the deportation of the Acadians in 1755! Mourn the hanging of Chevalier de Lorimier in 1839! Keep alive the memory of the ignoble Durham Report and the burning of Canada's Parliament by the English in 1849! O Quebec, France's eldest daughter! Hast thou remained true to thine baptismal promises? Like a mother, tend thee to the memory of Louis Riel, unjustly put to death by perfidious Albion, who still torments thee to this day! Remember the infamy of Regulation 17, which did banish French from the schoolrooms of Ontario! Remain faithful to memory's calling and to the apostolate of rancour!
—200 days of indulgence

On the back of the prayer, Jeanne had printed a picture of herself sitting at the wheel of her van, arms outstretched, as though about to clutch a child to her breast.

"It's yer duty to remember. You can start by studying this. There'll be more to come."

Jacqueline shyly raised a hand to inquire if the second history lesson might touch on the horrors of Papa Doc's reign in Haiti. Heather suggested they might consider adding a line by which to remember the dead of the War of 1812 in her very own Essex County. And so, a whole cortège filed through Jeanne's home, a procession of the dead, the executed, the crucified, the dispossessed, the enslaved, the crooks, and the oppressed from every corner of the world. They were up to their knees in the blood spilled by the cruelty of humankind. Perdita hadn't said a word. And it wasn't for a lack of horrors of her own. In her lifetime, she had witnessed the bombing of Zîb smack dab in the middle of the winter cabbage festival. She could have harkened back, too, to the public hanging of the Great Guru by the Soviets in 1945. But Perdita held her tongue. Jeanne's smile faded as she listened to the girls' suggestions. They could all feel the tension rising like a tide. There was no way Jeanne was going to include memories from outside Quebec as part of her duty to remember. Not for the first time, Rosa opened her mouth without thinking.

"You know, Jeanne, you called your prayer 'I remember' and you want me to learn it by heart. But even though I'm sure all those things really did happen, and they shaped our society today, I think it's a bit of a stretch to say that I remember them. If no one had told me about them, I wouldn't remember them at all."

Jeanne pursed her lips.

"It's *our* collective memory! That's why you have to remember."

"Jeanne, please, don't get all worked up! All I'm trying to say is that all those memories were given to me by
someone else. The way I see it, it's more a list of the horrors of war and of racism than anything else. Honestly,
Jeanne, who really remembers all that stuff? Who lived
through all of it? None of us! We're all here under one
roof and—"

"You *are*. Under *my* roof! And those are *my* memories!"

"But Jeanne, do you really think we can all live
together by making a mantra of all the abuses committed against the people of Canada? We could include the
horrors of Haiti and the terrible War of 1812, like Heather
and Jacqueline suggested. Why stick to the suffering of
just one group? The whole thing frightens me."

"Frightens ya? *You're* frightened? And what about us...
I mean, what about the poor people of Quebec City, when
they saw the English arriving with their machine guns in
1918? D'ya think they weren't frightened? And when we...
I mean when *they* saw the English ships appearing on
the horizon in 1759, don't ya think they were frightened?
Now you listen here, girl: if you dunno where yer from,
then you'll never know where yer going."

"Jeanne, calm down. Please. You make it sound as
though you were there, like you were actually attacked
by the English yourself."

"Don't you tell me to calm down, Rosa Ost! Take my
advice and learn what's there to be learned. D'ya hear
me? Cheese Whizz! And that goes for the rest of yiz, too!
I've had it up to here, bustin' a gut to educate you lot. Y'all
can go to hell!"

Jeanne slammed the door on her way out. Jacqueline took Rosa's hand.

"*Je me souviens*," she thought out loud. "You see those words everywhere you go here. *I remember*. It's like an obsession."

Perdita emerged from her silence.

"Where I come from, our motto is 'I forget.'"

How could anyone ever come up with a motto like that? they demanded.

"After Guruistan regained its independence in 1991 and right up until it recently broke up, the country went back to its old motto. Every car licence plate, every school, every coin bore the engraving 'I forget.' It's the solution Guruistan came up with to allow all the groups that make up the nation to live in harmony. After the Act of Forgetting of 1898 was imposed by the Great Guru, people were no longer allowed to refer to past wars and abuses without good reason. History books were expunged of anything that might reignite old grudges and jeopardize national unity. By 1925, the Act had met its goal: everyone had forgotten everything. Without proof, no one in Guruistan could accuse anyone else of wrongdoing in the previous century. The Act of Forgetting was amended in 1931 with the Clause for the Future, which gave the Great Guru the right to cherry-pick from the past to ensure a peaceful future for the nation. The country was resolutely, and legally, focused on the future, and the prophecies of Shah Gidogstori became its constitution. Anyone who insisted on wallowing in the past was looked down on, and liable to be accused of treason."

"But... I mean, the Great Guru literally turned you all into zombies!" Rosa spluttered.

"It worked wonders for the country's politics. A land once torn apart by tribal infighting enjoyed two decades of peace and economic prosperity from 1925 to 1945, just as Europe was sagging beneath the weight of its past. The Soviet invasion brought the good times to an end in 1945, but in twenty years of blissful ignorance, we achieved linguistic, economic, and cultural unity."

Upon arriving in Quebec, naturally enough Perdita had been surprised to see *Je me souviens* everywhere, a slogan that, although written in the first person, carried a clear imperative. She thought it would probably have been more honest to write "Remember!" rather than hide behind a supposed collective memory that was full of pitfalls and ripe for conflict.

As Rosa rode the number 55 bus to work, all she could hear was the hateful yapping of the evening she'd just spent, playing on a loop in her head. She began to dream of a distant future where a new generation had developed the ability to hermetically seal the two orifices that for centuries had been an open door through which too many words had infected the mind. Those happy, smiling people strolled through cities where justice reigned, closing an ear the way we turn a blind eye today to the absurdities of our existence. In that world, contempt no longer bred contempt. In that world, you only had to close your ears to get away from Renard and Jeanne Joyal. At the first note of discord, at the first snide remark, those people would retreat into deafness, no longer compelled to fight back against every noisy assault, at peace with the world.

Like she did every evening, she found a vague comfort in the bus driver's smile as he picked her up from the usual stop. "Hi there, Rosa! Feels like snow, eh? It's pretty chilly out." It *was* cold. The impenetrable, static cold that comes so naturally to Montreal. But you'd have to be a real optimist to think it was going to snow, Rosa thought. "Don't you think it smells like snow?" There was, truth be told, a smell hanging in the air, a smell that Canadians can sense like sharks sniffing out their prey. Not so much a smell as a fragrance, a promise that opens up the sinuses and the mind, a scent that hangs in the air just before the first snowfall in November. The empty bus sped through the darkness. A motley crew of students got on at the corner of Mont-Royal, each wearing a red armband, some sporting berets that had a red star pinned to them. Rosa thought it must be a mirage. There were at least thirty of them, chatting away, works by Chomsky and Marx under their left arms. Long hair and layered scarves. Maybe she had been forced to endure an evening of hell at Jeanne's just to be treated to this sweet solace before heading in to work? Maybe there really was a God. Rosa grinned at the students, who responded in kind. Comrades at last! Finally, Montrealers who wouldn't think she was crazy because she spoke to strangers! The guys had goatees, the girls had nose rings. None of their heads had seen shampoo in weeks. All the seats had filled up. A boy Rosa's age, visibly the leader of the pack, sat down next to her. She couldn't contain herself any longer.

"Good evening, comrade!"

The boy laughed.

"Hi!"

"My name's Rosa. I love your red armbands. Where can I get one?"

The boy grinned and opened his bag to hand Rosa a diamond-shaped piece of red felt and a pin. She immediately pinned the felt to her left sleeve.

"Were you protesting?"

"Yeah, we're from FUCQU, the Federation of Unruly Colleges and Quebec Universities. We're organizing a student strike all across Montreal. I'm Samuel-Xavier Blancheville-Tourangeau. Nice to meet you."

"Good to meet you, Sam!"

"Samuel-Xavier," the student corrected her sternly.

Rosa's eyes lit up.

"You're striking? What are your demands?"

"Haven't you seen the newspapers? The Quebec government wants to hike annual tuition fees by twenty dollars per student to pay for new libraries. It's totally gratuitous. Once again, students are being made to pay for the negligence of the generation that came before them."

"Which libraries?"

"I dunno. I don't go to libraries."

"Aren't you a student?"

"I am, but I'd rather buy my books."

"Ah... that's one choice, Samuel."

"Samuel-Xavier."

"Whatever. So, has your group managed to make the masses aware of your struggle? I think that's very noble

184

of you. I'm sure the Federation of United Construction and Other Factories and Fabricators (FUCOFF) would be able to give you some valuable advice about launching a revolution."

"Construction workers? Hmmm... I'm not really sure we have much in common."

"I'm wondering, Samuel-Xavier, whether you're inspired by the student protest movement in France or perhaps by an older tradition based on a more global vision of the universal right to education?"

"I couldn't tell you. It's Gillian-Rose Benedict-Davies who takes care of that side of things. She's the real head of the group."

"Will you introduce me? I'm fascinated."

"I'd love to, but she's on vacation."

"On vacation?"

"Yeah, she's burned out from her sociology studies. She's taken a week off to recharge her batteries."

"To recharge her batteries? Where? On an American campus?"

"Nah, Cuba. Varadero, I think."

Rosa was puzzled.

"And what's she doing there?"

"Oh, she went there with Proserpine-Nathalie Giroux-Minou to one of those all-inclusive hotels."

"Giroux-Minou?"

"Yep. Her mom's the writer, Michou Minou. She supports us, too. She's a big name to have on your side."

Rosa felt her heart deflating, like a child who's absolutely positive they'll be getting an electric train set on

Christmas morning, only to wake up to a box of hideous itchy wool sweaters.

"And where are you all going now?"

"We're heading back home to Saint-Bruno-de-Montarville. I have to study for my accounting exam. We left our cars at the Longueuil metro station."

"Your cars? I thought you'd be living under bridges, in parks, under overpasses?"

"Are you kidding! Those guys can't even be bothered to read Chomsky. They don't go on strike. We left our cars in Longueuil cause we're afraid they'll get stolen in Montreal. This city is so working-class. Turns out, the metro isn't so bad. You can sit down and enjoy your coffee... fair trade coffee, of course."

"You said you had an exam. Aren't you on strike?"

"We are, yeah. But we still go to exams. I mean, we don't want to flunk our semester at business school."

The bus had reached Sainte-Catherine, and the group of protesters piled into the metro station. Samuel-Xavier waved goodbye to a bewildered Rosa. It was then that something strange happened. Rosa shed a tear and, finding nothing else to wipe it away with, used the red felt armband. She then blew her nose noisily into the cloth, rolled it into a ball, and flung it into a back alley, where it landed between two discarded syringes. Her brusque steps increasingly resembled Jeanne Joyal's no-nonsense trot as she made her way to the Butler through the air filled with white promise. There, ten showgirls were waiting for her, thirsty for herbal tea and funny stories. They had to settle for herbal tea. Given their protégée's long face, by tacit agreement the girls rose and trudged up to their rooms in silence. Only Shu-Misty stayed behind.

"You look out of sorts, Rosa. Even your herbal tea tastes bitter tonight."

Rosa burst into tears. Shu-Misty held her in the embrace she'd learned from her late grandmother, a silent hug that calmed even the most heart-rending sobs. Rosa bawled as she held her head in her hands, her elbows resting on a pile of financial statements of an Ottawa-funded brothel that seemed to taunt her.

"I just don't get it, Shu-Misty. I don't get anything anymore. Nothing is real. I feel like I'm speaking a foreign language in my own country. I think I'm reading one thing, then it turns out to be the opposite. None of the signs are true."

"I think your problems stem from the fact that you all speak languages that have an alphabet."

"What do you mean?"

"The system you use to represent written language is limited to combinations that can only lead to misunderstandings. Twenty-six letters come up ridiculously short when you're trying to bring across the full complexity of human relationships."

"Well, what are we supposed to do? Speak Chinese to each other?"

"I don't want you to do anything at all. It's already too late."

"Are you really trying to tell me, Shu, that Chinese ideograms would make it easier for us to understand each other?"

"It's simple. To the Chinese, you see, writing is made up of signs that are rooted in reality."

Shu picked up a pen and a piece of paper.

"For example, in Chinese, this pictogram means *rain*."

"It looks like raindrops falling on a window! That's brilliant!"

"And I'm not done yet. This one means *snow*."

"See, Rosa? There's rain at the top, then another picture below it that means *hand*. Snow is rain you can catch with your hand! It doesn't matter if you speak Cantonese or Mandarin, everyone understands. Whereas with you lot, as soon as *snow* becomes *neige* or *neige* becomes *snow*, you're lost. That's your curse. You took the easy route and went with the alphabet, and now you have to live with the consequences."

Rosa remained pensive. She gazed at the Chinese snow without being able to find any meaning in it.

"Sorry, Shu, but that just doesn't hold up."

"What do you mean? It's perfectly simple! Don't you see the snowflakes? Do you need a photo or what!"

"Those are supposed to be snowflakes? Snow never falls straight down, for a start. It twirls and swirls, it stings your face like little acupuncture needles. If you want to show snow, it should fall like this."

188

Rosa grabbed the pen from Shu-Misty's hands and clumsily drew the following character:

Shu took the pen back.

"No, not like that! The lines have to be nice and straight! And you forgot the hand."

"Well that's just it! How come you're so sure that snow is rain you can catch in your hand? Where I come from, we'd say that rain is snow that trickles between your fingers. Give me that pen back!"

"You're trying to teach *me* Chinese now? You've got some cheek!"

"What about *you*? Since when does snow fall in straight lines?"

The two women examined the sheet of paper that was now covered in Chinese snow and rain, both determined to impose their own vision of the weather on the other. Someone outside on Saint-Laurent shouted: "It's snowing!" Shu-Misty and Rosa looked up to see thick snowflakes falling in straight lines. Heavy, sticky snow. Eager to drive home her point, Shu-Misty went out onto the sidewalk and stood with her hand outstretched, letting a centimetre of snow build up on her fingers as she looked Rosa square in the eye through the window. Once the evidence had been gathered, Shu-Misty retired to her room without another word. Rosa stood behind her counter and cried too many tears for her hand to hold.

When a girl from the Gaspé Peninsula realizes that she no longer even understands how snow falls, all she can do is cry. Because at that point, she no longer understands anything. Not a thing.

The snow didn't last. Twenty minutes later, the wet streets of Montreal had regained their November sheen. Rosa cried all night. All that remained of the whole sorry episode was a daily balance sheet spotted with dried-out tears and covered in Chinese pictograms.

In the early hours of the morning, Rosa finally gave in. She called Mayor Duressac, the only person in Notre-Dame-du-Cachalot who had a phone at home. She let the phone ring twenty-nine times. Long enough for the mayor to emerge from a dream in which he and Terese Ost had been dancing a sensual tango. "You loogg so pretty tonight, Terese. In that lobster-red dress, beneath the star-filled northern sggy, your eyes shine ligge the lights of Baie-Ggomeau from the port in Matane... I love you ligge belugas love the ggold, I love you ligge puffins love the shrimp that the tide washes up at their little webbed feet," he mumbled, drooling into his pillow. So who could blame him for mistaking Rosa's voice for Terese's? He was stunned.

"Mr. Duressagg, it's Rosa, *sniff*..."

"Ah! Rosa! It's you talgging to me in the dargg. But wait! Rosa, you're ggrying? Things didn't turn out too well for you there, eh? Well, it's not surprising: what do Montrealers understand anyway, apart from hoggey and fries?"

"Mr. Mayor. I have to talgg to Aunt Zenaida."

"Why, of ggourse, my little Rosa, of ggourse. I'll go and wagg her now!"

"Wag her?"

"No, I mean I'll go and get her. But what time is it in Montreal?"

"It's twenty past five in the morning. It's early, I know, but I just ggan't tagge it anymore, Mr. Mayor."

"Stay right there, Rosa!"

The old lady was sent for. It took twenty minutes. They had to wake her, then they had to rouse Napoleon to drag her, kicking and screaming, out of her bed and over to the town hall. But as soon as she heard the voice of her darling little Rosa, old Zenaida calmed down and stopped clawing at Napoleon's ears. Rosa spoke nonstop for a good five minutes. She talked about her Wednesday evening, her friends' insults, the history lesson, meeting the so-called socialists of FUCQU, the mystery of Chinese pictograms and how she still hadn't found the wind, and a litany of other hardships that the old woman listened to without so much as a raised eyebrow. When Rosa's sobs had finally died down, old Zenaida barked, "You can't make a silk purse out of a sow's ear," and hung up, eager to return to her still-warm bed.

CHAPTER 6

The Great Upheaval

IT WAS THE TALK OF THE VILLAGE: Zenaida had been sent another letter from Montreal. The foghorn sounded, summoning everyone to the parish hall. Mayor Duressac could barely contain himself. Four villagers were dispatched to fetch the old woman, who was refusing to leave her rocking chair. The strapping young men transported the reluctant knitter to the hall, where the villagers were waiting impatiently. Duressac noticed that, sadly, half the seats were empty. Boredom had struck several times since the last missive. The reassuring howl of the wind in the parish hall's rafters had given way to the lamentations of the grieving families. "It better be good news this time!" said Napoleon, handing the letter to Mayor Duressac. Trembling with emotion, the elected official sliced open the envelope with a flick of a lobster claw and began to read.

Montreal, November 30, 2000
Dear Aunt Zenaida,
I've put off chegging the Butler Motor Hotel's Oggtober financial statements until tomorrow night. I'd rather give you my news before I go ggompletely ggrazy. I sleep so little that sometimes I wonder how my body ggan stand it. I hope you're well and that you're snug and safe in our little wooden home. I got your postggard. Aunt Zenaida, you ggannot imagine how happy it made me. I ggeep it beside my bed so I ggan enjoy the ggomforting sight of your handwriting when I wagge up just before supper. I see the stamp has La Boldugg's piggture on it. You sure know how to pigg me up. Sometimes I'll sing a song or two of hers to give me strength when the nights at the hotel get too long. Jasmine and her friends—I told you about them in my last letter—thingg I'm very funny with my La Boldugg songs. They even want to worgg one into their routine at the Nile! Ggan you imagine, Auntie? Our musiggal heritage from Gaspé a hit with performers in Montreal!

An indignant voice piped up:
"And what about our wind, eh? Here we are droppin' ligge flies and *mademoiselle* is off singin' La Boldugg!"
Impervious to the attack, Duressac went on reading.

I must admit I'm a little out of sorts these days. I didn't want to bother you with my problems, so I didn't men-

tion that I've been seeing someone for a few weeggs now. He's a police officer with the Montreal police department. He's... an Aggadian.

The same annoyed voice piped up again:

"Oh, so now she's seein' city boys, is she? Well, isn't that just fine and dandy!"

"Ggome on, it's only natural," a woman's voice retorted. "She's as sweet as ggan be, our little Rosa. Of ggourse the men have an eye on her. And she has needs, just ligge everyone else."

Another voice, blessed with an uncommon gift for concision, added:

"Yeah!"

Duressac clicked his tongue, a smile playing at the corners of his mouth. Little Rosa was the spitting image of her mother at that age; he couldn't dispute what he'd just heard. Memories of his youthful union days with Terese Ost raced from one ear to the other. Old Zenaida had stopped her rocking upon hearing the news, and she smiled, too. Purple and pink memories of one particular evening in 1891 flooded her mind. Duressac continued to read:

Anyway, this friend recently aggompanied me bagg home and received a frosty reception from my landlady. I haven't seen him since. I never thought to asgg him for his phone number, so I ggalled the police station to tragg him down. They asgged for my name, then told me that ggonstables didn't tagge personal ggalls at worgg.

195

So, I wrote him. He Freplied right away, sending a note to the hotel:

"My dear Rosa, I thingg it would be best if we never saw each other again. I'm not da man you're loogging for. Réjean."

Unhappy with his reply, I wrote him another letter, asgging why he had abandoned me. Once again, it didn't tagge long for him to reply:

"My dear little Rosa, I ggan barely say the words, but I won't be able to see you again. You must not write to me, either. I guess dat is dat."

The indignant voice spoke up again:

"I guess *dat* is *dat*? What ggind of way is that to talgg! What the hegg does the Aggadian mean?"

The mayor picked up where he'd left off:

"... I guess dat is dat. This is striggly between you and me, but your landlady sent me a very worrying letter. And I quote:

'Monsieur Savoie, I am writing to inform you of a situation that weighs heavily on my mind. My name is Jeanne Joyal and I run a home for young women in Villeray. For a number of weeggs now, I have been renting a room to a young Gaspé girl whom you have met. This young girl was entrusted into my ggare by the Psygiatrigg Institute where she was ggommitted for three years. I often receive boarders from the world-renowned institution. Rosa suffers from a very rare psyggiatrigg disorder: she believes herself to be

the reinggarnation of Rosa Luggsemburg. Patients who suffer from this terrible affliggtion often deny the ggondition and will agguse those who are trying to help them of lying. It would therefore be pointless trying to help her. Being in a relationship ggould very well worsen her ggondition. The doggtors who put her into my ggare to help her find her feet again asgged me to support her, to proteggt her, to watch over her ligge a mother. The slightest shogg to the system ggould unsettle her, plunging her into an abyss from which she might never reggover. And so, I would be most grateful if you ggould help us with our treatment and ggut off all ggontaggt with her. I have spoggen with her doggtors and we all agree it would be a shame to have to inform your superiors of the situation. Thangg you for your ggollaboration on the matter. Yours sincerely, Jeanne Joyal.'

So, you see, Rosa, I don't want to ggompromise your reggovery, or my ggareer. I hope dat you get better soon. I'll never stop loving you. Réjean."

The audience scratched its collective head. Even Mayor Duressac wasn't sure what to make of it all. He went on:

So, you ggan imagine my despair, Auntie. I ggeep reading Réjean's letter over and over again and I ggan't believe it. How ggould Jeanne say such a thing? Why did he believe her? I don't dare ggonfront Jeanne with the letter and betray Réjean's ggonfidence, but more than anything I'm afraid she'll ggigg me out on the

*street and I'll end up living in a tent under Highway 40
with all the students who ggan't afford a place to live.
My heart is broggen and I ggan feel the violence rising
up inside of me, something I would never have thought
possible.*

All I ggan do, Auntie, is go bagg to my aggounts.

Your despairing Rosa

December is the cruellest month for the Montreal soul.
The orgasm of fall colours gives way to a dreary requiem of
grey. Rosa stood behind the front desk at the Butler watching people file past on the sidewalk. Some had clearly been
taking imported substances to brighten up the dullness.
Others clung to an arm that would haul them all the way to
December 8, the Feast of the Immaculate Conception, by
which time snow would, with any luck, have shrouded all
the ugliness in white. And yet, besides a notable chill in the
air, the forecast held out little hope of a white Christmas
that December 2000. It had even rained a time or two.
Cold, sluggish rain that fell in straight lines. Struggling
to break out of her funk, Rosa went back to her financial
statements in the back office. She no longer felt guilty for
not recording Gillian and Cassandra's comings and goings.
After tallying up the amortizations, prepaid expenses, and
the cost of electricity, heating, housekeeping, and salaries
(her own, plus Sri's day salary and the other evening salary), Rosa had long since realized that the hotel was one
of those businesses that was always in the red, its owners
having left it to its fate in order to write off a taxable profit
elsewhere.

Cassandra, the bookkeeping lady of the night, had to explain the concept of cross-subsidization to her: offsetting a loss on one activity with the profit from another. The loss-making Butler was being kept afloat by the operations of a profitable company, in this case, a shipping company. Rosa couldn't help but apply the notion to human relationships. The people who love us so much, the ones who serve us up on a silver platter all the affection we could ask for, make up in a way for all the ruinous relationships we have. A smile from Aunt Zenaida, in other words, helps offset the spitefulness of others. "Yeah, it's a bit like that," Cassandra smiled.

The owner of the hotel, a man from Ottawa, by all accounts, insisted on remaining anonymous. He would never know that in three months Rosa had indirectly profited from Gillian and Cassandra prostituting themselves to the tune of six thousand dollars. Six thousand dollars in twenty-, fifty-, and one-hundred-dollar bills that Rosa had stuffed into a shoebox and hidden under her bed. Six thousand dollars' worth of crime, lies, and degradation that, like the pea beneath the princess's one hundred mattresses, left her tossing and turning all night, disrupting her sleep, refusing to let her rest. The accumulated wealth, far from bringing her satisfaction or making her feel in any way proud, prevented her from looking Terese's photograph in the eye and from holding the giant winkle to her ear, for fear of the motherly disapproval she might hear. Ill-gotten gains seldom prosper.

Rosa held her head in her hands. The exhaustion of weeks of fruitless toil, the despair at not finding the wind, the harrowing tension on Rue du Saint-Ciboire, and Savoie turning his back on her weighed heavy on her shoulders. She'd come to realize she wasn't cut out to be a decadent. She plugged her ears so as not to hear the protestations as the dregs of the Nile spilled out noisily onto the cold sidewalk. In her state of unimaginable fatigue, the slightest sound shredded her nerves. The drunken grumbling of Jasmine's audience was particularly grating that night. Rosa realized in horror that she no longer felt as though she belonged to herself, that her work had become mortifying, alienating. A Gaspesian tear landed in the heavy silence, right on the line "Cash on hand at the beginning of the year." A firm hand grasped Rosa's shoulder, and she jumped in fright. It was Suzie and Mimi, the two voluptuous showgirls from once socialist Africa, come back from the Nile. They stood before Rosa like two Nubian queens.

"We wanted to say goodnight, Rosa. We're exhausted. We're off to bed," Mimi purred, her voice like a lioness on the savannah.

"Wait a minute. Are you crying, Rosa?" Suzie asked. "Are you all right, my little gull from the east? Did someone hurt your feelings?"

Mimi clasped Rosa's head tight against her breast while Suzie stroked her hair. Rosa closed her eyes and thought how there wasn't much difference between the sub-Saharan embrace and the times Terese and Zenaida would cradle her in their arms whenever Rosa had a toothache, an ear infection, a bad dream, or any of the other afflictions of childhood. The girls sat down beside Rosa as she wiped away her tears.

200

"I think it's time for a story," Suzie said, giving Mimi a wink.

"I think you're right," Mimi replied.

"One day at school, this very keen teacher, a European guy, gave us an assignment to write a poem."

"Such a pain in the ass."

"Oh yeah."

"Can you imagine, Rosa, what our homework was? 'Write a traditional African story of your choice in verse.'"

"That guy was crazy."

"Totally crazy. People had been telling the story we're going to tell you now for hundreds of years without worrying about rhymes or having to count syllables, and it was just fine like that. Everybody was perfectly happy. Then this little white man shows up and expects us to change everything. It had to rhyme."

"He gave us 4 out of 20 because our story wasn't in quatrains."

"He never said he wanted quatrains! He said he wanted a poem."

"He thought he was so smart."

"But we did give him a poem."

"It goes like this."

As serious as could be, Mimi and Suzie chorused as one:

There was a giraffe from Mozambique,
Who was terribly, terribly chic.
But try as she might,
It never looked right,
When she wore her new scarf at the creek!

The two Africans gave her a smile and went up to their room. The limerick had left Rosa perplexed. She'd never thought of herself as a giraffe. In fact, she'd never spent time comparing herself to any creature from the animal world. If anything, she would have been drawn to the pelican, when, in the evening mists, he returns from his travels abroad to his nest of reeds. But what did Alfred de Musset know of terminal Boredom? How can a poet get the wind to pick up? Her conscience had been calmed for a second time. She had only to share her spoils to counteract the old saying that "ill-gotten gains seldom prosper."

::

As Rosa continued to tumble into unhappiness, back in Notre-Dame-du-Cachalot, Zenaida's knitting needles are clicking in time to Beethoven's Sonata No. 8. Clickety-clack. Only the sound of the plastic needles tapping against each other breaks the grim silence that lies over the house. She glances up at the clock that has just reminded her of everything she hadn't given a thought to since May 28, 1914. Outside the sea is slack. The distant, heart-rending shriek of a tiresome gull. Shut up, you horrible creature. It's December 7 in Notre-Dame-du-Cachalot. The sun's first rays have just turned the easternmost reaches of the village pink. The sound of knitting needles has suddenly stopped. Zenaida has leapt to her feet. Dropped on her still-swaying rocking chair, the unfinished sweater lies like the shed skin of a snake. Zenaida strides purposefully through the still-sleeping village. Her little arthritic fists manage to rouse Mayor Duressac from his slumber, surprised to find the old woman beating at his door in the dead of night. Standing there in his pyjamas, his eyes still in the other world, his mouth pasty, he doesn't understand what Zenaida is gesticulating wildly about as she yanks on his sleeve, barely giving him time to pull on his rubber boots and his anorak. Let's be clear about one thing: even with no wind, the Gaspé Peninsula is absolutely freezing in December, especially at dawn. The drop in temperature has had a calming effect on the Boredom. Its particles crystallize in the cold, settling in clumps around the lethal geyser instead of floating unimpeded through the air in search of innocent victims. Zenaida and Duressac walk past the source, which is now surrounded by a thin crust of crystallized Boredom, a snotty yellow bordering on bile-green. A careless Arctic tern has landed on top of it and is desperately struggling to free itself from the stinking slime. Zenaida and Duressac ignore its cries as they hurry along. The old woman pushes on into the half-darkness, dragging the mayor behind her by the sleeve. She grows agitated as they arrive before the Three Sisters. As Duressac looks on in horror, she begins to remove the stones that make up the second sister.

"Zenaida, no! Don't disturb the sleep of the—well, uh, you know what I mean."

As the December 2000 morning dawned, Duressac was reluctant to exhume Madeleine Barachois, the unfortunate woman who, thirteen years earlier, had tried in vain to escape the wrath of the villagers. The old woman began grabbing hold of the stones and removing them one by one, urging Duressac to join her in the desecration. Some were small enough to be held in one hand, while others required more than a grandmother's frail arms.

"Zenaida! Whatever's the matter with you? You're gonna bring us nothing but trouble."

Duressac began to laugh. What else could possibly befall him now? He'd just buried Terese, the only woman he'd ever loved in this wretched world, apart from his mother. For years he'd been promising a socialist paradise to the embittered locals who lived in his run-down village and now they were dropping like flies. Little Rosa, like a bottle at sea, had yet to send back any encouraging news from Montreal, and now old Zenaida had gotten it into her head to dig up the remains of Madeleine Barachois, at the risk of making the pair of them, on that calm, early December morning, the villagers' latest target. No, things couldn't get any worse. Desecrating a grave was the only thing left for it. As he pondered how long it would take for him to succumb to a hail of rocks, Duressac took off his anorak, rolled up his pyjama sleeves, and began to help the old woman. They would soon reach the centre of the pile of rocks. The sun was now up. The tide was rising. Rocks were flying in every direction. Their hands bloodied, their brows slick with sweat, Zenaida and Duressac took in the sad sight. On bended knee, eye sockets trained on a salvation that was never to come, Madeleine Barachois' skeleton emerged before them. There was no doubt it was her: Duressac recognized the wedding band that hung loosely from the ring finger on her left hand. Gravity alone kept her round, silver-rimmed glasses balanced on her skull. Arm outstretched, the skeleton held up a small stoneware pot that had once contained a Christmas cactus. The pair moved closer to the pot, only to discover, much to their amazement, that the cactus had survived being buried for thirteen years. Not only had the plant survived in the pitch darkness, it had thrived. As everyone knows, to get a Christmas cactus to flower, you just need to keep it in complete darkness for three weeks in October, then move it into a shady spot and water it every day. It seemed to the pair of them as though the cactus had sucked all the life out of the woman. Hundreds of pink buds dangled from the end of its branches, threatening to burst into flower at any moment.

"Inggredible," Duressac gasped.

"If you want something done right, do it yourself," Zenaida added.

Slowly, she moved in close to the cactus and plucked it out from the bare bones that Madeleine had raised to the heavens. She tucked it under her arm. Zenaida hobbled off back home, where she promptly gave up on knitting and took up gardening instead.

The villagers woke that morning to find the mayor on the beach, busily rearranging the stones that covered the second sister.

"The birds must've knogged them over," Miss Nordet reasoned.

The villagers each found an invitation tacked to their door. Penned by a hundred-year-old hand, it summoned them all to the parish hall at 6 a.m. sharp on December 7 for an extraordinary meeting. In place of a signature, all it said was "Bundle up!" The villagers trudged over to the parish hall at the agreed time, quite certain they were in for another public reading from the mayor of a letter from Montreal in which they would learn that Rosa was married, pregnant, or goodness knew what else. But they were in for a surprise on that cold and blue December day as they took to their plastic seats. The curtain was drawn over the stage. The darkness of Advent. Silence. A murmur. Then, an invisible hand pulled on the curtain. There on the stage, on an oak stool lit by a single spotlight, sat a massive Christmas cactus, its branches sagging under the weight of hundreds of little buds that were threatening to burst open. The murmur faded away. Voices were raised.

"It's a Ggrisstmas ggaggtus!"

"Just ligge the one Madeleine Barachois used to have!"

"And it's about to flower!"

"But where did it ggome from?"

"Loogg at all the little buds."

Footsteps slowly made their way across the boards. A stooped silhouette advanced through the penumbra, carrying a watering can. Water flowed out of its mouth and down onto the cactus. The silhouette set the watering can down on the floor and clapped twice. A blinding beam of white light slowly descended from the ceiling and stopped ten centimetres from the cactus. Five minutes passed. Nothing. Then the silhouette again clapped twice. One by one, the buds opened slowly as the tearful villagers looked on in delight. Everyone held their breath. Hundreds of magnificent red flowers opened one after the other, like stars in a promised sky. Someone let out a sob. The curtain closed over the apparition. The villagers returned home beneath the cobalt sky. The cold had crystallized the Boredom so thoroughly that it was no longer lethal; it was nothing but a lingering bad smell.

::

In Montreal, fatigue, sadness, and despair had left our little Rosa drained of her last remaining ounces of youthful exuberance. Some dark and distant corner of her psyche had helped her suppress her memories of the short-lived promise of an idyllic life with Réjean Savoie. In forgetting, she had made the motto of Guruistan her own, confirming that sometimes the answer really does not lie within. She would barely think of him at all. Sometimes, whenever she would see a patrol car pass by, she would peer inside, just in case it might be the redhead, but her conscience had already made it clear to her that even if it had been, she wouldn't do anything more than watch him drive away. Perhaps it was for the best, she'd tell herself, to let Savoie, Notre-Dame-du-Cachalot, and any desire for change just slip away. She's barely recognizable, our little Rosa, on this early December day. She's lost weight. She no longer has the strength to stand up to the slightest thing. Some of Montreal's kinder souls would advise her to leave, to get away from Rue du Saint-Ciboire, but where would she live? That November, Heather, half dead with home-sickness, had raised the possibility of breaking her lease, but Jeanne had refused all attempts at negotiation. "A contract is a contract. For once an Ontarian can keep her word!" Her flat-out refusal had forced the other boarders, who had been harbouring similar aspirations, to abandon any dreams of freedom. Winter was coming. There might have been no wind, but it was winter all the same, and no one much felt like camping outside in Lafontaine Park or heading off to live in one of the dark suburbs, where television was the only release. It was as though the girls had been entitled to a certain amount of laughter for the year 2000 and had used it all up. There were only three gloomy weeks left and then the year would be over. That evening, Jeanne had to go out for work, leaving the whole house to the four boarders, who decided to hide themselves away from the rest of the world in Perdita and Rosa's room. Rosa told them all about her misfortunes, and how hard it was not seeing Réjean Savoie again. Perdita tried to cheer her up a bit.

"You know, Rosa," she began. "Your whole thing with Réjean doesn't surprise me at all. Where I come from, everyone knows there's no point dreaming of men and women living in perfect harmony."

"And how come you've got it all figured out?" Rosa asked.

"It's all down to Zîb."

"Zîb?"

"Yes, Zîb. It's the main town in Zîbistan, one of Guruistan's eight provinces. About three hundred and fifty thousand people live there. It's the world's leading producer of winter cabbages."

208

"Do they eat a lot of them?"

"They have a different winter cabbage recipe for every day of the year. Cabbage rolls, sauerkraut, cilantro cabbage, red wine cabbage, and more."

"And they eat it every day? It must smell lovely there in the evenings."

"They don't call it the 'Powderkeg of the Caucasus' for nothing."

"I bet. I just hope the wind's still blowing over there."

"The thing is, Zîbbers aren't as green as they are cabbage-looking. They're quite... well, let's just say that we in the capital find them somewhat peculiar."

"How come?"

"Zîbbers, you see, suffer from two strange conditions. All the men are colour-blind. They can only make out shades of grey, so they see everything in black and white."

"How sad!"

"They really couldn't care less, though. The thing is, their wives can see all the colours, just like everyone else. They spend their time describing everything they see to their brothers, husbands, and sons. Just imagine trying to describe the difference between the milky white of the moon and the immaculate white of lily of the valley to someone who can't even tell blue from red. It's not easy. Zîbber men will often give roses to their sweethearts, but they can't tell if the flowers are pink, white, red, or any other colour. Sometimes a man will be seen giving a woman he'd love to jump straight into bed with a bunch of white roses, which are a sign of chaste and pure intentions. The women know all about the handicap, but they suffer in silence and struggle to figure out what the men are really trying to say."

"Oh dear!"

"I know! You should see the ones who don't have a woman at home to help them out. They walk around town dressed in the most garish outfits. One grey sock, the other royal blue. The insides of their homes might be painted any old colour. An orange rug with apple green walls."

"My God. And what did they do to deserve that?"

Heather and Jacqueline were fascinated.

"No one really knows. Back in the days of the Soviet Union, when Guruistan was still under communism, dozens of Zîbbers were sent to the gulags for flying a huge black flag they'd thought was red for the May Day parade. They were arrested for being anarchists."

"That's awful!"

"Why didn't they just ask a woman? If you want something done, ask a woman!"

"But all the same."

"Mind you, Heaven did a job making up for it. Zîbber men might be colour-blind, but they all have the voices of angels. Morning, noon, and night, they sing the loveliest songs."

"Ha! That must help them make up for the white flowers."

"Yes, but there's one problem."

"What's that?"

"All of the Zîbber women suffer from amusia."

"From what?"

"Amusia. It's a kind of musical disorder."

"I'm not following."

"They can't recognize or remember a tune. They can hear a succession of notes, but they're completely tone-deaf."

"Ah! OK! Like Che Guevara. He suffered from that, too. He couldn't make head nor tail of music, couldn't recognize a tune. It's sad, all the same. So, the women haven't the first idea about music?"

"Nope. They all speak with monotonous nasal voices. You'd think you were at a civil servants' meeting."

"And they can't hear the Zîbber men sing?"

"They can hear them, but they forget as soon as it's over. They're completely incapable of appreciating it. *The Wheels on the Bus* and Verdi's *Addio del passato* are all the same to them."

"That's tragic!"

"And that's not all... If you can believe it, the women of Zîb are all wonderful artists. The city walls are covered in unimaginably beautiful paintings. But the Zîbber men see them only in black and white. So, when a woman paints a colourful painting to express her love for a Zîbber man, he'll just give her a polite 'thank you' and send her a dozen white roses."

"Haven't they ever considered same-sex relationships?" Heather interrupted.

"It makes no difference, Heather," Perdita laughed. "There are just as many same-sex couples in Zîb as there are anywhere else, but they don't seem to be any happier. The men spend all day correcting each other: 'No, no, no! It's a G sharp. That's a G you just sang! Could you please try a little harder?' while the women squabble about what colour the sky should be in a spring painting: 'You put far too much yellow in that cloud. It looks like it's about to pee.' It never ends."

By now the girls were holding their heads in their hands, thoroughly disheartened by the fate reserved for the good men of Zîb, whose glorious songs were either lambasted or ignored, and for the women, whose wonderful paintings were either unappreciated or disparaged.

"Do they ever manage to have children?" Rosa wondered. "There can't be many left, by the sound of things."

"They manage," Perdita replied. "Their children come into the world unhappy, condemned to repeat the ways of their parents. They spend their days listening to their mothers trying to describe the finer points of an impressionist painting to their fathers. Then, when evening comes, it's the fathers' turn to describe arpeggios and harmonies to wives who don't understand the first thing about music."

Listening to the trials and tribulations of the people of Zîb hadn't helped bring Rosa's smile back. The answer might not lie within, but it was depressing all the same. She stared silently at the floor, as the others felt a mix of compassion and pity for her. Heather was looking pensive.

"You know, Rosa, that red-haired Acadian guy of yours, maybe he's just a red herring, a diversion. Maybe he's distracting you from what you're really looking for."

"I don't know, Heather. Don't you think it's a bit mean to call him a red herring? Not everyone from the Maritimes is into fishing, you know."

"No, but it can't hurt. Think about it. I'm quite sure that Réjean Savoie is nothing more than a red herring in this whole story. Think about it, Rosa. You left your village on the orders of a giant winkle, you became friends with a bunch of prostitutes and an international troupe of topless dancers, you wound up here with us, you found the courage to stand up to Jeanne... Don't you think all that's complicated enough without Savoie getting involved? You've seen more things happen in three months than most get to see in a lifetime. Now that, my friend, no matter what you say, is a revolution. A personal revolution, I grant you, but a revolution all the same. I've been watching you, Rosa. I think you're amazing. You're pretty damn cool. This Réjean guy doesn't deserve you. Trust me, he's a red herring. Just a red herring. This whole story doesn't need a Réjean Savoie. Let him rot in hell!"

Rosa let Heather's comments sink in. A red herring, really? Of all the creatures living in the bottomless sea, herring, even when smoked, had never been her favourite. She much preferred tender pink shrimp, firm cod, and the little snow crabs that Terese used to boil every spring. Were a red herring to find its way onto her plate, she thought, she'd think twice about eating it.

The girls were silent. Then Jacqueline, sensing more waterworks, stood up.

"I wrote a little something," she confessed.

The girls perked up.

"Well, what are you waiting for? For us to all die of a broken heart? Go get your story!" Perdita ordered her.

Jacqueline rummaged around in a notebook and removed three sheets of paper covered front and back with her fine scrawl. They listened the way the people of Israel listened to Moses on his return from Mount Sinai.

"It's called 'The Dwarf'."

"Go on!"

"Read it!"

"Get on with it!"

"Krik?" Jacqueline cleared her throat. "Krak!"

The Dwarf

Once upon a time in the city of Vicenza, a dwarf named Emilio married a woman called Maria, who was also short in stature. They had both grown up to inquisitive looks and cruel gibes from the people of Vicenza. Even though they both came from important and influential families, all their money couldn't buy them peace of mind or an existence away from the prying eyes of their fellow citizens. Every day, curious onlookers from as far away as Bergamo filed beneath their windows, eager to see the strange couple with their own eyes. Maria eventually succumbed to a severe bout of melancholia. "Husband, I cannot so much as go for a peaceful stroll through the streets of my own city. This is no life. Only yesterday, as I was walking through the market, I felt a hand on my shoulder. It was the fishmonger who wanted to touch me, to make sure I wasn't one of those automatons they talk about in books. The Chinese silk of my dress still reeks of the whiting she'd just been scaling. I can't bear it any longer, Emilio." Emilio was saddened by

Maria's tears. He asked her not to leave the house while he came up with a solution to their problem. Emilio, whose family name was known throughout Veneto and all the way to the Papal States, decided to put the problem to his father, a fabulously wealthy spice merchant. The head of the family suggested that Emilio remove Maria from the city's petty clutches. As required by the fourth commandment of the Holy Catholic Church, Emilio decided to follow his father's sage advice and have a splendid villa built in the Venetian countryside. The sumptuous home was ready to welcome the Lilliputian couple on the Sunday after the Assumption of the Virgin Mary. So as not to spoil the surprise, Emilio blindfolded Maria and helped her into a carriage drawn by two magnificent chestnut horses. When they reached the villa, he unbound his wife's eyes and she was stunned by so much beauty. Emilio had spared no expense, employing the finest architects in the land. The villa was surrounded by a huge garden, which was itself circumscribed by a thick stone wall several metres in height, and decorated by the most beautiful frescoes imaginable, each picture representing a world inhabited only by dwarves. Around a well-set table, a diminutive Christ presided over a Last Supper with his dwarf apostles. In the surrounding garden, a pint-sized Venus and Ganymede stood guard. Stretched out on the lawn, there was even a diminutive Hermaphroditus sculpted from the choicest marble. Maria burst into tears.

"Oh, husband! You have built for me a paradise on earth! Your love for me knows no bounds."

Maria was not wrong. Emilio had even gone so far as to employ only dwarfish servants. From the chef to the gardener, right through to the stable boys, all the employees were dwarves.

For two years, Maria and Emilio lived blissfully in their made-to-measure home, far from the hurtful stares of the city folk. Servants took care of keeping the house supplied with everything they needed, and Maria never again had to subject herself to the stares of others.

One day, God answered Emilio's prayers: Maria was with child. The couple were overjoyed. Maria gave birth to a beautiful little girl, a dwarf just like her parents, confirming that life in the villa would continue to be perfect. They called the child Francesca. The little girl grew up dressed in silk. Private tutors—all of them dwarves—were summoned from Austria and Rome. Emilio hired artists to make dwarves of the characters in her fairy tale books and appointed renowned authors to rewrite the stories in order to reflect the image of the world he wanted his daughter to have. And so the child grew up in a dwarfish Eden, turning twenty without ever suspecting the reality outside the villa's walls. One morning, however, as Francesca was picking bay leaves in the garden and singing an ode to the Virgin Mary, a cavalryman passed by on the other side of the wall that stood between her and the truth. He heard the young woman's voice and immediately brought his horse to a standstill. He was charmed by the purity of the disembodied voice. So, he wrote a note, which he put in a bottle and lobbed over the wall. The message landed at Francesca's feet, an impassioned note penned in florid Italian. A meeting was requested. Until that day, never before had she suspected that anyone at all might have existed outside of her father's estate. She could no longer sleep, her thoughts occupied by her mysterious admirer, who would come back at the same time every day and beg to meet her. Fearful and delighted in equal measure, eventually she replied to the note and arranged a meeting with her suitor at midnight on the Feast of St. John the Baptist, on the very spot where she had so charmed him with her singing. There in the darkness, her beau cast her a rope ladder and she climbed to the top of the wall, where, lightheaded, she fell into her admirer's arms. In the place of the woman he had imagined, he found himself clutching what appeared to be a cruel trick of nature. Dismayed and appalled, he rode his horse at a gallop all the way to Vicenza, where he abandoned the little woman by a fountain. Francesca came to at dawn, just as the fishmongers were setting up their stalls in the market square. What she saw left her transformed. She had landed in a city of colossal and unimaginably ugly creatures. She ran through the market shrieking like a lunatic. An old woman reached out and grabbed her by the shoulder. It was the same fishmonger who had traumatized Maria years earlier. The smell of the low tide emanated from the old hag, who informed her in malodorous Italian, "Why, yer the spittin' image of yer mother!" Horrified, Francesca ran all the way to the outskirts of the city, tears streaming down her face. All around her, she saw huge statues and towering people and, faced with the lie that was her existence, her childhood crumbled away. A man working in the fields caught sight of her and realized she must be from the dwarf estate just outside the city. He dropped her off there, and the young girl ran up to her room in dismay.

217

*Crushed by the whole ugly truth, she sliced open her veins
with a golden dagger. That night at around eight o'clock,
her parents found Francesca in her white dress, bathed
in blood. Clutching her daughter's mortal remains to her
bosom, Maria smelled the sad whiff of whiting from the
fishmonger who, twenty years earlier, had left her disgusted
by all Creation. Francesca was still clutching a note in her
right hand. "I am too small and they are too big," she had
written. Overcome by grief, Emilio and Maria would burst
into tears on the stroke of every hour, and eventually ended
their days in the paradise that had become a prison to
them. After their deaths, the villa was sold to a nobleman,
who named it 'Ai Nani.'*

Jacqueline's room echoed with quiet sobs. Heather
had buried her face in Perdita's shoulder, while Rosa had
got to her feet, so as not to die of sorrow in her chair. No
one said a word. Rosa left the house on Rue du Saint-
Ciboire to catch the number 55 bus, while the other three
boarders headed to their beds, trying to rid their minds of
the image of the dwarf girl. That night, all three dreamt
the same dream. They were running through the streets
of Montreal. It was the St. John the Baptist holiday, and
everyone was staring at them.

No one brought up the literary incident the following
morning. Each of the girls, even Rosa, found a reason
to identify with Francesca. The Gaspé girl compared
her fate to the dwarf's, wondering if putting up walls
around young children was a good idea. Heather was
more motivated than ever to learn French.

Francesca hadn't died in vain.

Decades later, when she breathed her last on the shores of Lake Erie, Heather's last words came from Jacqueline's story: *"Je suis trop petite et ils sont trop grands."* I am too small and they are too big. No one in Essex County, where even the sparrows of Point Pelee sing in English, knew why the last words of Heather Smith, née Fischbach, were in French.

Things often look better in the morning, just as it is clear to all that Truth does its best work at night. On the evening of December 7, the old adage that it's best to sleep on it did little for Jeanne Joyal's girls, who tossed and turned in their crisp clean sheets. Insomnia had them in its grip. Perdita sat up straight in bed, twenty minutes after Rosa left for work. "Twenty to midnight," she sighed. She could hear Heather's sobs from the next room, and felt a twinge of guilt. Feeling sorry for her, she pulled on a long bathrobe and a veil to cover up in and slipped out onto the landing, a clear breach of their landlady's curfew. Jacqueline had beaten her to it. The three women began to exchange tissues and kind words. Jacqueline offered her sincerest Creole apologies to Heather, who was staring out at the street from the window. What she saw there brought the sobs to an abrupt end.

"Jeanne's van is gone!" the Ontarian yelped, with one final sniff.

"No way. Where would she go?" the Haitian retorted.

"Look, I'm not dreaming. The van was there earlier this evening."

The skeptic and St. Thomas checked for themselves, and indeed it was true. Either Jeanne had gone out, which meant that the girls would now be living in constant fear of flying pigs, or some ruffians had made off with their landlady's van, entirely oblivious to the risk they were running. The second scenario brought a smile to their lips. They tried to picture Jeanne, reduced to taking the subway. They went downstairs. The ceramic *Parti québécois* key rack hung as usual by the door. Jeanne's keys weren't on it. There was no two ways about it: Jeanne hadn't come home.

"Do you know what I think, girls?" Heather smiled. "I think it's high time we had a little fun around here."

Perdita replied, ever the rational one.

"What? You want us to dance to American music? What if she comes home without warning? She'd just go on and on about language politics."

"Actually, I was thinking of something else..."

Heather made her way along the dark hallway, as stealthy and graceful as a cat. She felt for the handle on the door to the forbidden room. It was locked.

"Ah! Locks are like Jeanne's laughs. They can be forced!"

The girl from Ontario went to work. Heather—whose arrival in Montreal had coincided with a series of break-ins at the Windsor Hotel—darted back to the kitchen to grab the tools she needed. Armed with a butter knife, a hairpin, and an eraser, she got the better of the lock standing between the girls and Jeanne's privacy in less time than it took to say:

"Are you out of your mind? What if she comes back?"

"We'll hear the van's engine from miles away. We'll have plenty of time to get out."

The door creaked and opened onto the landlady's lair.

::

Meanwhile, back downtown, a sorry scene awaited Rosa. It had all started with a shout that had gone up from Cassandra on the cold Saint-Laurent sidewalk: "Run! It's a raid!"

On the stroke of midnight, a dozen police cars and paddy wagons screeched out of the darkness to block off the boulevard between Sainte-Catherine and René-Lévesque. A crowd gathered at either end of the blockade. Troy was burning. Rosa elbowed her way towards the hastily erected barricades. A voice rose high above the commotion.

"It's a raid. They raided the Nile."

An army of police officers stood outside the Nile, supervised by none other than Réjean Savoie. Into the police vans they hustled the club's patrons one by one, as they attempted in vain to hide their faces from the journalists' flashbulbs. Conservative MPs, clergymen, and drunk students were singing, "*Vive la Canadienne! Vole, mon coeur voooole! Vive la Canadienne! Et ses jolis yeux doux...*" Rosa's heart split in two when she saw Lenin's Great-Granddaughters file out in their costumes, handcuffed like dangerous murderers. Propelled by the fission of every atom in her heart, she kicked out at the shins of the constables who were trying to hold her back. "Let me through!" Rosa broke through the line of police officers and ran straight for Savoie.

"What do you thingg you're doing? What the hegg is going on?" she raged.

"Excuse me, miss? Move along, please. You're in da way."

"Réjean, the girls didn't do anything wrong. Listen to me!"

"Miss, if you continue to stop us going about our work, I'll have to arrest you, too."

Rosa was petrified. She no longer recognized the man who used to come by to pick her up after her night shift and made her feel as though she counted for something. Réjean was riding the crest of a power tsunami, and had left Rosa washed up on the shore, all alone. It was at that moment that Rosa realized once and for all the gulf that separated her from the gesticulating uniform. She felt a sudden urge to gun down everyone who was there. It wasn't so much the painful breakup with Savoie that was driving her crazy as the fact that the seedy world she had called home since August was now crumbling around her. She had always remained at the fringes of whatever the showgirls and streetwalkers were getting up to, but she had felt part of that unconventional family. She had never forgotten that her mission was to rouse the wind, first and foremost. But she had gotten caught up in criminal dealings and African fairy tales, and could no longer tell good from bad. It seemed to her that Réjean hadn't realized that his little raid spelled the end of her career as receptionist and controller at the Butler Motor Hotel. What would become of her if she was out of work? Of course, she could always hope to find a job in a bookstore or a restaurant somewhere, but never again would she know the fierce friendship that had bound her to Jasmine and her gang. We can see where our little Rosa was coming from. Somewhere between the resignation of her village and the oppressive surroundings of Jeanne's house, the ladies at the Butler Motor Hotel had saved her from despair more than once, convincing her that she had a role to play in this strange world. It was while making herbal tea for a troupe of strippers who'd been worn out by a long night at the Nile that Rosa had realized her usefulness. Carlota and Roberta's talk on moral relativism, Suzie and Mimi's African limerick, and Shu-Misty's Chinese lesson had opened her eyes to the human condition more than all the pages of Marx. Her world was a huge brothel, and she was the madam. Réjean had just destroyed all of that, right before her eyes. The thought swirled around her mind like two lost snow geese in the Montreal sky. Rosa was breathing heavily. Turning her back on what remained of her self-control, she launched a verbal atomic bomb into the sky over Montreal, causing onlookers to turn their heads and take in the sad spectacle:

"FUGGGG!"

Over the hullabaloo, a police officer shouted, "The two hookers got away! They slipped right through our fingers!"

Savoie spat on the ground. He pretended not to know Rosa. A uniformed giant of a man grabbed Rosa by the waist and slung her over his shoulder. Biting. Kicking.

Scratches. Threats. Gaspesian shouts. Evil spells. Curses. The hysterical young woman was deposited back on the ground, where she was able to take in the regrettable scene that followed.

Savoie was freeing the exotic dancers one by one, putting each in a different car. The cars took off to a concert of sirens and a ballet of flashing lights. The bruiser holding Rosa told her the girls would be taken to the airport, where they'd be deported to distant lands. Jasmine, the sole Canadian, was the only one allowed to remain in the country. She was locked up at the penitentiary in Joliette, where she swiftly passed away from anger and sadness. Then suddenly Jeanne Joyal appeared out of nowhere, flashing a smile as she strode towards Savoie. There was a handshake. Rosa stopped breathing for the next hour and a quarter.

The agent explained to Rosa that the Montreal police force had been given the order to dismantle the troupe and arrest everyone in it. An influential minister in the federal cabinet had ordered them deported, and it was Réjean Savoie who'd been put in charge of the operation. He'd pulled it off brilliantly. There would be deportations that night like never before. And the sting wouldn't spare the Butler. The stretch of the neighbourhood from René-Lévesque to Sainte-Catherine would be scoured until everything, consciences included, was clean.

Shu-Misty went back to China. Rejected by all and condemned by her government for treason, she was sentenced to hard labour at a seafood-processing plant. There she was made to clean the squid and octopus that passed by her on a conveyor belt before continuing on to a machine that sliced and diced them with its enormous, sharp blades. Sickened by the stench that constantly reminded her of the painful passing of her dear grandmother, after two days of hell Shu-Misty closed her eyes, climbed onto the conveyor belt with the octopus, and waited calmly, not shedding a single tear, for the blades to free her forever from the seafood plant. Her body was chopped up into a thousand little pieces, packaged in tin cans, then sent back to Canada in the very same container that had carried her there the first time. In Toronto, a bejewelled food critic whose every word was treated as the gospel truth pronounced her absolutely delicious in sweet and sour soup.

Savoie had reserved a sad fate for Nelly and Blondie. Nelly was dispatched to Leipzig, where she moved back in with her mother and was out of work, out of work, and even more out of work until one day she was discovered obese, haggard, and catatonic in front of a rerun of the cult TV soap opera *Lindenstraße*. Blondie was sent to Thailand, where she became a bikini-clad server on the beach at Phuket until December 26, 2004, when she was swept away by an enormous tsunami.

Ludmilla and Tatiana were sent back to Saint Petersburg and Komsomolsk-on-Amur, Siberia, respectively. Devastated at the prospect of never seeing Shu-Misty again, Ludmilla threw herself into the freezing waters of the Baltic Sea from the deck of a cruise ship where she'd found work as a showgirl. Tatiana, meanwhile, forever separated from her dear Ludmilla, has been staring at the Amur ever since. One day she'll throw herself in, and her body will sink to the depths of the great grey river. Molecules from her sadness will disperse in the waters and, with a little luck, the currents will reunite the decomposed cells of Ludmilla and Tatiana somewhere in the glacial northern seas.

The Cubans Carlota and Roberta were deported to Havana, where they became tour guides for Quebec tourists who were thrilled to hear Montreal French being spoken under the Caribbean sun.

Savoie's sting operation had worked perfectly.

"It's about time this cancer was removed from the heart of our city!" the *Étoile de Montréal* wrote the next morning.

But the cancer had metastasized. All its cells had been deactivated or entirely eliminated, except for the two Africans. Suzie and Mimi had seen it coming. Deported to Mexico and Colombia, they'd walked and sung their way back to Montreal, arriving two years later to set up (discreetly and under a new name) an African dance company. They recruited a dozen exotic dancers from all across the Americas on their long walk back, picking up in secret where Jasmine had left off.

As for Sri Satyanarayana, he swore he didn't know a thing about any of it and set to work finding himself a new night receptionist.

CHAPTER 7

Immaculate Conception

ROSA GAVE HER DREAMS of Réjean Savoie the send-off they deserved. She made the motto of Guruistan her own and began to forget. The lanky redhead was buried in the mental cemetery alongside those who slam doors behind them and those who have been kicked out of Heaven. Rosa was young, so the cemetery still had only a few headstones. There lay Réjean Savoie, anyone who had ever treated Rosa with a lack of respect, and a particularly unpleasant little girl from Notre-Dame-du-Cachalot who one day chased Rosa along the beach brandishing a fistful of long, dark green seaweed that the children were convinced was alive and full of bad intentions. In their nightmares, the seaweed would wait until nightfall to spring to life and strangle its victims. The little idiot—her name was Marie-Claude Starfiche—had terrorized Rosa for days on end, until the young communist, backed into the deepest corner of her childhood fears, had scooped up a rock as big as her head and flung it in Marie-Claude's direction, hitting her square on the forehead and putting her out of action for a week. While the Starfiche girl had been left with no more than a tiny scar by which to remember the act of legitimate self-defence, it had also taught her not to go around getting her classmates all riled up, especially not when they were the children of people who were out to save humanity. And so forever after, Marie-Claude avoided making so much as the slightest eye contact with Rosa, who had promptly buried the irritating little girl in the Cemetery of Petty Squabbles, where she had lain ever since. As everyone knows, it is strictly forbidden, and absolutely pointless, to dig up the unfortunates who have met with this sad fate. The discord in Rosa's heart was absolute and final.

As our little Rosa continued to make her way in this world of ours, she would bury friends, distant family members, and colleagues until, by the time she reached her golden years, she would find herself with her own field of white crosses as vast as the many dotted across France since the Great War. It was there that the memory of Réjean Savoie now lay. It wouldn't be long before the little white maggots of oblivion had eaten him all up, leaving behind nothing but his sturdy frame and dazzling white smile. For a time, Rosa would stare after every police car that passed by, in the hopes of seeing her Réjean, trying to satisfy her unhealthy curiosity. Then, one day, she would stop looking at them completely. She would no longer even see them. Far off in the distant future, our little Rosa will open the *Étoile de Montréal* to learn that Sergeant Savoie has just been made head of the Montreal police force or has perhaps been fatally wounded during a routine operation, depending on how the gods are feeling or which way the tea leaves settle in the bottom of her cup that morning. Peering at the photograph of the fifty-nine-year-old man, she will react like a historian who has just unearthed a rusty Bronze Age artifact from the depths of Mesopotamia. She will spend a second or two wondering what use it might ever have served, before consigning it to the museum of memory.

We must confess that another solution was available to Rosa. She could have, at virtually no expense, sealed the red herring Réjean Savoie in a jar of vinegar in order to produce him, one day in the future, as proof of a past love. Plenty of others would have done just that. If visitors were confused by the jar of pickled red herring, she could have told them all about love at first sight, the Return of the Snow Geese, and Réjean's ultimate betrayal. But that would have meant that every time she recalled those events, she would rekindle her pain until it slowly petered out. She had no intention of cheapening the pain of her first love by trotting it out for the rest of her days to anyone who cared to listen. Réjean Savoie was dead and buried. Whenever people asked if she knew anyone in the police, she would always say she didn't. Whenever, by some misfortune or other, she would hear an Acadian accent on TV or the radio, she would turn it off. One day Réjean had told her, "It's not wot you have dat makes a body proud, it's knowin' dat you'll have it." Rosa would be proud enough not knowin' dat she'd ever have anudder ting.

One day, someone had written (Rosa could no longer remember exactly where), "Every time we read, we leave a little of ourselves behind." She was equally sure she'd once heard someone say, "To leave is to die a little." To her mind then, it was entirely possible she was already dead, and no one had noticed. Because there was no denying that up until this point, life for our little Rosa had been nothing but one long list of good books and goodbyes. No matter how she cut it, her body was already in an advanced state of putrefaction, and no one could have predicted the moment when she would stop dying. She'd started dying the day her mother had taught her to read in the little kitchen on the Gaspé Peninsula, and she would stop the night when, before going to sleep one last time, she would set down on her bedside table a book by which to light up the nighttime shadows. Because, as each of us knows, every line we read takes away a little piece of us and draws us closer to the very moment that was promised to us on the day we were born. But some of us, believing we have found the secret to a long life in the books we read, unwittingly advance our own deaths.

Happy people don't read stories.

Meanwhile, on Rue du Saint-Ciboire, Perdita, Jacqueline, and Heather had just cracked open their landlady's door and stepped into the biggest disappointment of their lives. Where they'd hoped to uncover an extraordinary secret, they found only a room with pale grey walls, a bed draped in a dark grey blanket, a greyish-green dresser, and, hanging above the bed, Christ on a steel crucifix, His arms stretched out in bone-cracking excruciation. The drapes were drawn, as faded as any memory, plunging the sad tableau into near darkness. A few rays of light from the dazzling street lamp outside cast a subdued halo over the scene. "It's like a nun's cell," Jacqueline whispered. As the other girls looked on wide-eyed, Heather opened the top drawer of the dresser. Perdita found the light switch, and the world's neatest drawer appeared before their eyes. A dozen pairs of socks were carefully aligned along the length of the drawer, each pair in a spot numbered one to twelve. Beside the bed, a grey-striped rug did its best to soften the no-nonsense, maple floorboards. "It's like a Zîb rug," Perdita murmured, lifting one corner. "Little grey rug, how old you are, how ugly you are, how tired you look. Where did you come from?" Jacqueline inquired.

The question disappeared into an ocean of insignificance once they realized the rug was covering a trapdoor. And where there's a trapdoor, there's a handle. The girls didn't hesitate for a second, pulling it open. The temperature in the room immediately dropped four degrees. Three centuries' worth of mustiness assaulted the three pairs of nostrils. Perdita backed away. "Girls, this is going too far. It's creepy, it stinks, it's just a trapdoor to the basement where she keeps her turnips and potatoes. There's nothing to see." But curiosity had robbed the other two girls of their sense of hearing. They were already squinting hard, trying to make out what lay beneath Jeanne's bedroom. No one keeps turnips underneath their bed. Jacqueline went out and came back with a flashlight. All they could see was a wooden ladder that stretched down into the void. Heather went first, followed by Jacqueline. Perdita was absolutely terrified and refused to go with them, preferring to keep watch. She'd had more than her fair share of hiding out in underground bunkers during the bombings that had marked her childhood and, ever since, she had harboured fusty memories of dark, cramped spaces.

Jeanne Joyal's basement turned out to be nothing more than a dank storage space, its walls shimmering with damp. A deadly silence reigned. Floor-to-ceiling shelves were packed with old bound books that oozed with mould. Some of the lettering on the bindings was still golden, spelling out titles of religious works that appeared to be largely devoted to the life of the Virgin Mary and countless histories of France. Rusty chests in an advanced state of decay stood in each corner, begging to be opened. The first contained a pile of letters bound together with string, some old cloth, bundles of wool, tools whose use had long since been forgotten, and, strangely, a small suit of armour. Jacqueline barely had time to stuff the letters in the pocket of her bathrobe when Perdita sounded the alarm. Someone was coming. Goosebumps. Catlike footsteps. The rustle of women's clothing. In no time at all, the three girls were sitting in Perdita's room while Jeanne Joyal, tired but proud of a job well done, returned to her room, determined to spend the rest of the night asleep.

A letter addressed to us is interesting. But a letter addressed to someone else is fascinating.

Upstairs, the girls pored over the letters, one by one. Some were so old that the paper cracked as it was unfolded. Others were only a few months old. Regardless of their age, each word whispered by Jacqueline from each piece of correspondence dropped like a bombshell. The girls pressed their hands to their mouths to stop themselves crying out. Teardrops fell by the dozen onto the giant winkle that Rosa kept on her bedside table. The mollusk was soon drenched in tears as salty as Windsor salt. Jacqueline translated into modern language the words that had been committed to the age-old paper.

Québec, October 14, 1671
Sister,
All the girls who came this year are married, aside from the bearer of this letter whom I commit to your establishment. Since I am in the usual ferment caused by the arrival of troops and supplies for hungry mouths and for the war, I have undertaken the honour to write to you concerning the girl who carries this missive and whom I believe best entrusted to your care. I am much obliged. Jeanne came over on one of the King's vessels, along with other girls to be married, and has shown none of the qualities required to start a family in Québec.

It will be my honour to describe to you her personal traits and to distinguish the fair from the foul. I must inform you that she knows not how to obey orders, that she tried during the crossing from Old France to command the crew of the vessel, and that the captain did try to throw her into the waters before the Isle of Anticosty. As her vessel approached Québec, it could be seen listing to one side, so eager were the passengers and crew to distance themselves from her. Although she is most disagreeable and hardly pleasing to the eye, I could not advise her to return to France as Monsieur Colbert has asked us to keep her here. The damsels who travelled with Jeanne have complained heartily about the treatment they received from her. While the girl has a diverting tongue, she knows not when to cease once her audience has been sated. It appears that Jeanne made every decision, from the distribution of meals to how the sails were rigged. No captain will agree to take her on board for France, for any sum of crowns.

Here in Québec, none of the settlers or tradesmen will have her for a wife, and it is beyond my authority to force a marriage. You are surely wondering why I am sending her to you in Montréal. All I can say is that Jeanne will be of no aid to the colony in Québec and I advise you to put her to manual labour since she has often shown great physical strength. I ask that you please accept Jeanne at your mission and shall have her remit to you the amount of seven thousand livres as a sign of my recognition.

I continue to believe that Jeanne might be of some use in Montréal. However, I implore you to make no mention of the English since the very word sends her into a rage that sets her to shouting in fury. I would add that this service rendered to your humble intendant will

be reimbursed in the future. Consider it an order of the
King to keep the girl with you.

I beg of you, therefore, to accept the humble thanks
of your most obliged, Jean Talon

The second envelope looked more official. Addressed to Jacqueline, it bore a French stamp and was post-marked several months earlier. It had been sent by none other than the leading French publisher, whose every publication had instantly catapulted its authors to the ranks of literary stardom.

Paris, 2 February 2000
Madame,
It is our great pleasure to inform you that our reading committee has unanimously recommended the publica-tion of your short story collection The Toad and Other Stories. *The strength of your writing and the on-point themes left our readers in no doubt. Please respond to this letter within two weeks in order to accept this offer of publication. Failing which, we will assume that the manuscript has already been accepted elsewhere.*
Yours sincerely,
Esther Winckler

In typical fashion, Jacqueline lowered her head and shed a tear or two. She didn't shout or scream. She didn't pound her fists against the grey walls of Rosa and Perdita's room. As she turned to face the window, her tears began to fall on the giant winkle. *"Penbèch la! Gad travay li,"* she murmured.

Perdita continued to go through the pilfered letters. Another dated May 13 informed Heather that Lester B. Pearson University in Toronto was offering her a coveted place in its constitutional law program. Needless to say, the deadline for accepting the offer had long since passed.

Perdita paused when she saw the third letter. Her shoulders slumped as she spotted the Turkish stamp and the return address. Penned in a bizarre alphabet, the letter's three paragraphs left the Guruistan native unusually silent. Her tears joined the salty stream that was falling on the winkle.

There were other less-important letters addressed to the girls, too: Christmas cards, birthday wishes from an aunt in Miami, and, last of all, a recent letter from Réjean Savoie. Perdita read it aloud, not suspecting that Rosa had just tiptoed upstairs so as not to wake her friends and was listening to every word from the other side of the door.

Montreal, December 5, 2000
Dear Ms. Joyal,
The Montreal Police Department would like to express its profound gratitude for the services you recently provided. The information that you passed on was invaluable in the Lenin's Great-Granddaughters affair, particularly in relation to their place of residence and the illicit goings-on at the Butler Motor Hotel, and it has been very helpful to me as I wrap up my investigation. The chief of police assures me that the favourable outcome will be my ticket to a swift promotion.
I will be eternally grateful to you.
Réjean Savoie

When they reached the end of the letters that were of interest to them, either because they were so old or because they'd been addressed to them, the girls fell silent for a long time. Rosa came into the bedroom and sat down beside Jacqueline on the bed. The winkle, now drenched in tears, gleamed in the dark. It began to give off a gentle hissing sound. Rosa brought the tear-soaked mollusk to her ear, listened carefully to what it had to say, set it back down on the table, stood up, and strode out of the room.

Jeanne Joyal was sitting on the edge of her bed, wearing the suit of armour that Heather and Jacqueline had found in the secret cache earlier. Jeanne seemed to be waiting for someone and smiled sweetly when Rosa walked into the dimly lit room.

"There you are at last."

"What's that supposed to mean? What's all this, Jeanne? What are you dressed up like that for? You look ridiculous. How can you be so deceitful? Do you have any idea of the harm you've done? You do nothing but hurt everyone around you. Everyone wants nothing more than to see you die a violent, painful death."

"There you are at last, my little Rosa. It'll all be over soon."

"Why are you talking like that?"

Instead of replying, Jeanne handed Rosa a piece of card. It turned out to be a postcard from Notre-Dame-du-Cachalot.

Everything comes
to those who wait.

Z.

Jeanne Joyal
8510, rue du Saint-Ciboire
Montréal (Québec)
H2P 2H9

"It's the same one I was sent," Rosa said, "only you got yours two days before I left home. You know Aunt Zenaida? She never mentioned you."

"Aunt Zenaida hasn't spoken for a very long time, Rosa. She was condemned to wander the earth, spreading proverbs wherever she goes."

"Condemned by whom?"

"He who shall not be named, Rosa. The one who calmed the wind. The one who saved me from the stake in exchange for my soul."

"That's why you went all the way to the Gaspé Peninsula to get me? It was me you were looking for?"

"Your mother raised you well. I was sure you'd grow up to be a good person. Now I have a favour to ask."

"You were 'sure'?"

"Rosa, I've really had enough. I can see the divine gift inside of you, a gift I once had, of staying a child. You get that from me, Rosa."

"I don't understand any of this, Jeanne. What's happened to your accent? Why are you talking to me like

238

this? What's with the armour? Why do you go around hurting everyone?"

"It's not *hurting people*, Rosa, it's what I have to do. They're orders, divine imprecations. You can't understand. When you've been alive for five hundred and eighty-eight years, you no longer see good and evil the way the young folks do."

"That's why you don't have a shadow?"

"Nothing at all, my dear. I'm completely transparent. Time has made me as translucent as glass. What people see is an illusion of me. Something that should have disappeared a long time ago. But it will all be over tonight, thanks to you, Rosa. Come here and let me give you a hug."

"Don't touch me! I came downstairs to tell you I'm leaving. I can't stay here any longer. I couldn't care less what happens to me now. I'll sleep under the Jacques Cartier Bridge, if I have to."

"Ah... Jacques Cartier... Now there was a great man. He deserved so much more than a bridge."

"Are you crazy? Have you been drinking?"

"Alcohol no longer has any effect on me at all. Sit down. Sit down and I'll tell you who I am so that you can at last understand who you are."

Rosa hesitated. The landlady's eyes shone with a fatigued brilliance. Rosa sat down next to Jeanne on the grey bed, beneath the metal crucifix, to listen to the strangest story in the world.

"Rosa, my little Rosa. I was born in 1412 in Domrémy. I—"

"Wow! How can you say that and accuse Jacqueline of writing a load of garbage? Will you listen to yourself? People have been committed for less, you know."

"Shhhh... Listen. You can see who I am, can't you? My name is Jean. What nobody understood back then was how easy it was for a slightly built boy like me to pass for a girl. I could put on armour, wear men's clothes... they still thought I was a girl. Everything they wanted of me, I gave. The rest, as they say, is history. The voices, the army, Orléans, condemned to death, the stake, yadda yadda yadda, everyone knows all that."

"But you're right here in front of me!"

"That's down to an error of judgment. You see, Rosa, once I was sentenced in Rouen, they put me in a cell and that's where He appeared to me during the night."

"He who shall not be named? Shah Gidogstori? Who?"

"Shhh... worse than that. I'm talking about the Prince of Darkness. I was afraid, Rosa. I was afraid of the flames. I was afraid of suffering. No one wants to die at nineteen, not even as a heroine, not even in 1430, and definitely not at the stake. So, he offered me immortality in exchange for my soul. I would have been crazy to say no. I signed the contract in my blood. An innocent girl was burned in my place and the crowd saw only smoke and flames."

Rosa laughed incredulously.

"My whole life, I've felt bad about that poor shepherdess. She hadn't done a thing to anyone and she got barbecued alive in the public square at Rouen for her trouble. The crowd wanted to see a virgin burn, and that's what they got. Immortality is what I got. Being eternal seemed like a good idea to me at the time in 1431, but I've had enough. The only way I could escape my destiny was to be killed by my own sword at the hand of one of my descendants. That's what He said. And that's where you come in, Rosa. That's what you're here for, just that. I had to be patient. Plenty of others would have killed me long before now. I really had to be as cruel as cruel can be."

"So you don't have a soul? That's why you don't have a shadow?"

"Yes, Rosa. That's exactly it. It's the soul that blocks the light. It's our soul that leaves a fleeting trace of our humanity on the ground. A shadow is nothing more than the outline of the soul."

"And after that?"

"For me? I lived all over France, sometimes as a man, sometimes as a woman. Whenever people began to suspect I wasn't getting any older, I would fake my own death and move to another town or village. One day, some time around 1670, I heard they were looking for volunteers to go to New France. I was already two hundred and fifty-seven years old by then. I'd seen it all before. I needed something new. Far-off new horizons. Some adventure. I pretended to be a poor little girl from the Hôpital de Paris and I took her place at La Rochelle on a ship bound for Québec. I've been wandering this cold and snowy land since 1671. Do you know what's a fate worse than dying, my little Rosa?"

"Let me guess. Living with you?"

"Oh, sarcasm! You've got your mother's wonderful sarcasm, Rosa... The same sarcasm she dished out to the bosses at the Petticoat Paper Company... No, Rosa. Never dying, that's what's worse than dying. Can you see how the years have left me bitter? But it's all going to be over soon. He had me sign it in my own blood. 'Your own flesh, in freeing thee, shall be imprisoned.'"

"Bitter? I think you're beyond bitter."

"Well, just you wait five centuries and you'll see that *a man is still a wolf to another man*, that we haven't made an inch of progress, that we keep on massacring, exploiting, raping, invading, stealing, killing, and you'll have had enough of life, too. You'll want to go back to the good old ways, you'll have had enough of people turning their nose up at your identity, you'll want to stop anyone and everyone coming across the borders into France!"

"We'll see how I feel in five hundred years, Jeanne."

"I can see that smirk. You think you know everything because your mother had you read Marx and Engels when you were eight, eh? You think things'll turn out different for you, don't you?"

"Tell me, Jeanne. Since you knew my mother..."

"I knew her better than anyone! And you, my little dolt. Ah! Do you deserve to know the truth, Rosa?"

Jeanne's armour creaked as she cackled.

"What truth?"

"Do you remember the evening of May 20, 1980, Rosa?"

"How could I? That's the day I was born."

"I remember it very well. I'd been in Notre-Dame-du-Cachalot for ten years. I'd met your mother. She was so young, so pretty, so full of life. Out to change the world. I was head over heels in love with her, Rosa. She didn't care that I looked like a girl. Terese could see what people were like on the inside. She knew how to bring out the best in them. She could see the good in everyone. She allowed me to forget that I was more than five hundred years old. She was the woman I decided to have you with. I'd never met a more delightful soul. I was over the moon when she told me she was pregnant. The end of my ordeal was finally in sight. I knew I couldn't help raise you. I knew that no one should have to put up with me. I know perfectly well how unbearable I am."

"What do you mean, 'decided to have me with'?"

"You still don't get it, do you? Your mother knew I was still alive. She told Zenaida just before she breathed her last. She gave her my address so that she could send me this postcard. I didn't just happen to be driving along Route 132 that day when I picked you and those horrible girls up."

"Horrible girls?"

"They have no self-respect! They make a mockery of everything your mother held dear."

"That couldn't be further from the truth. They give new life to those symbols, in a world that has forgotten what they used to mean. There's nothing wrong with taking your clothes off in public to the *Internationale*!"

"You stupid little girl."

"*I'm* stupid? Now you listen to me, you racist old witch. First you walgg out on me the day I was born. Then you ggome pigg me up just to magge my life hell. You let my mother die without a cent on the Gaspé

Peninsula while you're off living it up in the big city. And you have the gall to ggall *me* stupid?"

Rosa's anger took on Gaspesian proportions. She took a few deep breaths. That was it. She couldn't take another word of it. It all came spewing out in one foul green stream. The young socialist felt the resistance of politeness falling away. Rosa raged. And this is what happens when a Gaspé girl spends all her time hanging around Montreal with sex workers.

"Listen, you old bitch. You've spent months driving us up the friggin' wall with your boring talgg of the Office québécois de la langue française, your ggan't-sing-for-shite ggrooners, your stupid historiggal soap operas, and your obsession with history. You've been magging life miserable for four girls who want nothing more than to support themselves, and now you're ggalling me 'stupid'? Bring it on, you old shrew, you bullying old harridan. You want me to ggill you, is that it? Is that what you want, bitch? You ggruel, evil, wringgly old ogre! You disgust me. You magge me sigg. Fugg you!"

"Would you do that for me, Rosa? Would you do that for your father? Would you take my sword over there and cut my head off?"

Rosa stood up. Without a word, the corner of her lip well and truly raised, she grabbed the sword with both hands from where it had been resting against the wall. Although she had no idea where she found the strength and skill to handle the freshly sharpened blade, she swung it around three times and as her roommates, who'd been drawn downstairs by the shouting, looked

244

on in disbelief, she decapitated Jeanne Joyal, whose head dropped to the wooden floor with a thud. From the landlady's neck, where you might have expected to see a spurt of blood, there came instead a hiss of foul-smelling gas that robbed the girls of their appetites for a full two weeks. It was the stale and pungent smell of five hundred years of wanderings and misdeeds. The girls were dumbfounded, unable to take their eyes off the severed head as they breathed in the putrid air.

"How are you going to explain this to the police?" Perdita asked.

On the bedside table, the winkle had just split in two, having waited all that time for salty tears before speaking again. It was now useless, and was thrown out with the garbage the following morning.

Rosa caught her breath. Having lost her mother and now killed her father, the young girl could feel a Freudian turn coming on. For a split second, she felt compelled to gouge out her own eyes with the sword. But they had to get rid of Jeanne's body.

The murdered landlady, her sword, and her head were awkwardly packed into her van. Heather got behind the wheel, and the four girls took to the road. Rosa's voice had changed. She no longer spoke in the happy-go-lucky tone the girls had always known.

"Now that's what I call a feckin' revolution, girls," she said.

The Jacques Cartier Bridge offers the best views of the city. But on the night of December 7, 2000, any sightseer who had cared to look down over the Old Port, which lay empty on that glacial December night, would have been treated to the strangest of sights. In the freezing, stock-still night air, the murderer and her sidekicks had used the sword to fix Jeanne's head back onto her body, not unlike an olive on a toothpick on top of a sandwich. It had been Perdita's idea. No one survives the horrors of the Caucasian wars without learning a trick or two. As they struggled to contain their nervous laughter, the girls shoved what remained of Jeanne Joyal, Montreal landlady, pyrophobe, former *fille du roi*, heretic condemned to be burned at the stake in Rouen, and royal pain in the ass, into the river with a loud splash. She was off to swim with the fishes in the polluted waters of the St. Lawrence. For weeks, they would feed on her decomposing flesh only to die of indigestion, washed up by the dozen on the shore, their bellies swollen. The pollutants that floated in the filthy water would eventually wear down the suit of armour. Only the stainless-steel sword would come to settle on the murky bed of the river by the city formerly known as Ville-Marie, now Montreal, world capital of smoked meat.

The landlady was gone, consumed not by the flames of Satan, but by the fish of the St. Lawrence.

At the very moment when Jeanne's body touched the water, the girls felt a draft of air on the back of their necks, a kind of ice-cold breath. They didn't dwell on it. After a stroll up Mount Royal, where they silently admired the city at their feet, they realized they were in it up to their necks. What were they going to tell the police? How would Rosa ever make it through an interrogation, especially if it was Savoie asking the questions? It was Jacqueline's fertile imagination that came up with the answer. The girls had realized that Jeanne had no friends and even the neighbours steered clear of her, so likely no one would notice she was missing. Once you've lived for five hundred years, you no longer know a soul. A letter of resignation was sent to the Office québécois de la langue française. No one called back to try to talk her out of it. The girls decided to stay on at 8510 Rue du Saint-Ciboire, so as not to arouse suspicion. It was Cassandra who agreed to bribe the notary in Villeray to draw up a fake will and transfer the property rights over to Rosa. The poor man—whose wife was a devout Catholic—was a regular of Cassandra's and didn't need to be asked twice.

The city woke to the Feast of the Immaculate Conception to find a terrible snowstorm raging outside. Trees, sidewalks, and cars were nothing more than white silhouettes. The wooden house on Saint-Ciboire creaked in the gale.

There was still no sign of the wind in Notre-Dame-du-Cachalot. On the evening of December 7, the villagers didn't eat a thing. The women sobbed. The children sought the company of animals. It was around midnight that the first creaks were heard. First came the odd rattle in the rafters, which might have been put down to the wooden beams shifting in the cold. But soon there was no doubt. The chimneys in some of the homes struck up an aria to life itself. The villagers shivered with cold. A little. They trembled the way some people do when they orgasm. Then they slept. But how were they supposed to sleep with all that racket? Roof tiles were ripped to shreds. The men nailed down wooden boards to cover the gaping holes left behind by the wind, while the women stoked their fires.

And the snow. Heavy snow, sticky snow, small flakes, huge flakes, blowing snow, loose snow, drifting snow. All night long.

The snow stopped the next morning. The wind hadn't died down. A westerly gust. The air above the St. Lawrence was as pure as the ten virgins from the gospels. In the villages scattered along that coastline of paradise at ridiculous latitudes, winter arrives like a relative who makes us dread every visit but who sure can spin a yarn. It sweeps in like a gossipy old aunt who requires constant tending and monopolizes everyone's attention, but who could imagine the calm beauty of summer without her? Winter is the uncle with a drinking problem who turns up unannounced with a two-four and has everyone in stitches for the first hour; the uncle who is witty, who dances and swaps apple pie recipes, then somewhere between the seventh and eighth bottle turns into a monster, his every beer-fuelled outburst leaving the women in tears. In Notre-Dame-du-Cachalot, it was the start of winter. They sang. They cried. They chased each other around in the whiteness. Everything was buried under thirty centimetres of packed snow that reflected the sun's rays back up like spears into the screwed-up eyes of everyone who had survived the outbreak of Boredom, the pungent whiff of which would never be known in Notre-Dame-du-Cachalot again. Dressed in an orange anorak,

Napoleon was running around in every direction, wailing like a madman. Gone was his camera. The covered bridge was all white, as were the Three Sisters. There was absolutely no way to make out the names on the letterboxes. And what do we see here? Goodness, we do believe Miss Nordet just cracked a smile! Arms spread wide, standing atop a rock buried in snow, there she is, grinning at the west wind.

Duressac collapsed into everyone's arms. Hugs and kisses were exchanged for the rest of the day. The village was jubilant. A lilac-mauve splotch could be seen making its way through the white mass. It was Zenaida. Wearing the same getup she'd had on the day Terese and Rosa found her in the block of ice on the shoreline, she walked purposefully towards the tip of the snowbound peninsula with the villagers in tow. The lifebuoy from the *Empress of Ireland* hung around her wrinkled old neck, shining in the Advent light. When she reached the edge of the freezing-cold waves, she turned to face the villagers. Then, in her age-old voice, she serenaded them, looking each in the eye. The song had been long forgotten, but the words came back to one and all as soon as they heard the opening bars.

"I'm on my way, I'm on my way,
But there's no need not to be gay.
My heart is light as day,
Now I'll be on my way."

With the strains of that impromptu winter chorus still hanging in the air, Aunt Zenaida—a woman who over the course of her existence had never uttered a single word that wasn't laden with wisdom—waded out into the icy waters of the Gulf of St. Lawrence with a smile on her face and disappeared in among the salty waves, whales, icebergs, and seals.

She was never seen again.

::

The sun had just risen over 8510 Rue du Saint-Ciboire. Rosa stood smiling on the balcony she was now officially the proud owner of. Jeanne Joyal had left Rosa everything she owned. Standing in the fresh January snow, Rosa was reading Jacqueline a letter she had received from back east.

> *Notre-Dame-du-Cachalot*
> *January 3, 2001*
> *My dear little Rosa,*
> *On behalf of everyone in the village, I would like to express our heartfelt gratitude for your generosity. The six thousand dollars you so kindly sent us will make up the funds we were lacking to buy the new wind turbine. To be entirely honest, we took five hundred dollars from your gift to replace the lamp in the lighthouse, which hasn't lit up the gulf since you were born. Every time we see the light we'll think, "That's thanks to our little Rosa!"*
> *Ever since the wind returned to Notre-Dame-du-Cachalot, there seems to have been one piece of good news after the next. Don't think for a second we're disappointed you didn't manage to rouse the wind—as*

long as it's blowing, that's all that matters. But you should have seen the looks on their faces when the cactus began to bloom! Wherever did Aunt Zenaida get her green thumbs? The cactus is now in my office, back at the town hall. We're making sure it has everything it needs. We've even ordered a few more from the gardening club in Rimouski. By making sure one of our twelve cacti blooms at regular intervals, we'll be able to keep our wind turbine turning all year round.

It's very sad you have elected to stay in Montreal, even though I'm glad to hear you decided to take over from that poor landlady of yours who disappeared so unexpectedly. I can see why you've grown so fond of the girls you wrote to us about in your letters. I'm sure they're equally fond of you. You may have thought you were in Montreal for the sole purpose of saving the fate of your village, but in reality you were busy writing your own story. It feels good to be in charge of your own destiny, doesn't it, Rosa? I always knew you would. But isn't it extraordinary, all the same, how Jeanne Joyal left you her whole house and everything in it? I mean, she barely knew you. She left you a big, clean house, its doors open to anyone. You should be very grateful. She must really have loved you. No matter what happens to the house, I hope you'll manage to take care of the boarders as well as Jeanne did—perhaps, if you still have enough of Terese's pluck and Zenaida's wisdom in you—even a little better! That said, I do wonder if renting Jeanne's room out to Cassandra really was a good idea. Do you think Jeanne would have approved of that kind of girl sleeping in her bed? But there you all are. Together. I can just picture you all cooking, swapping stories, sharing your troubles. I hope you will help the girls who have come from so far away to love this land of ours. May the sense of humour we Gaspé folk are renowned for light up your winter nights in the big city! I hope you will find a thread on which to string all those pearls of yours! Never forget where you come from, my little Rosa! May the currents of the St. Lawrence sweep you out one day into the fine blue gulf, where we will all be reunited in a spirit of joy and fraternity.

I've also enclosed a cheque that should bring a smile to your face. As you asked, we put your childhood home up for sale and, much to our surprise, it was snapped up less than ten days later. It's funny, isn't it, Rosa, a girl in Montreal getting sent money from the Gaspé Peninsula? We sold your house to a couple from Montreal, nice enough folks who came by yesterday to sign all the paperwork. Your little red shingled house will be their summer home. It seems the lady of the house has had enough of hot summers in the city. She'll be comfortable here. Do you remember, Rosa, the passage that your mother pointed to just before she died?

"Hegel remarks somewhere that all great world-historic facts and personages appear, so to speak, twice. He forgot to add: the first time as tragedy, the second time as farce."

Take care you don't become a farce, Rosa!

We'll build the first wind turbine behind your old home with a bronze plaque of your mother, yourself, and

Aunt Zenaida on it. We'll write your names in red and, just above that, we'll put: "He who sows the wind shall reap the whirlwind." I'm fairly sure that's what Zenaida would have said!

Your mayor, now and always,
Nicéphore Duressac

Jacqueline looked her square in the eye.

"Your accent's completely gone, Rosa."

Rosa smiled, then looked up to see Heather, Cassandra, and Perdita putting up new curtains on the upstairs windows. They waved to each other. On the immaculate white January snow—the light, powdery kind that doesn't stick to leather boots—Jacqueline's long silhouette stretched out before them, black and elegant against the cold, white carpet. No one noticed that the Haitian shadow was all alone. Only Rosa had noticed that, for a few days now, her body no longer cast a shadow.

They would eat winter cabbage that day for lunch, stuffed with canned squid from China. The rest of the afternoon would be spent playing Scrabble. It would be Rosa who collected the last "Triple Word Score" to empty her rack. Eighteen points, plus the letters her boarders hadn't managed to get rid of. Because Rosa had finally learned that one day we all get to count.

QC FICTION

Current & Upcoming Books

Visit **qcfiction.com** for details and to subscribe
to a full season of QC Fiction titles.

MIX
Paper
FSC® C100212

Printed by Imprimerie Gauvin
Gatineau, Québec